WHAT'S YOUR PROBLEM?

GEORGE ONSTOT

ISBN: 988157160
ISBN-13: 978-09881571-6-3

This is for A.M., who has taught me so much.

ALSO BY GEORGE ONSTOT

Bullies on Juice
Macho Fellows
Entrepreneur
Survivor Types
Native Grrl

CONTENTS

Moonshot   1

Fortunate Ones   53

Beer and Toilet Paper   81

The Son and the Moonie   105

Poor Boy   123

Bad Reggie   189

Right Place, Right Time   247

Sophie's Choice   283

Marge   323

What's Your Problem?   349

i

Moonshot

I'll drive you to the moon, Marge said, shaking a fist at Reg. She loved that threat: I'll drive you to the moon with one punch. The word moon came out of Marge's mouth slowly, like a cow lowing: Mooon. Reg, visual and imaginative, felt attracted to the spectacular and ludicrous; instead of being afraid, he asked himself, literally: How could she drive me to the moon? He pictured Cape Canaveral and worldwide TV crews. On the launch pad stood Marge and Reg as lab-coated technicians spoke of torque, velocity and wind shear. They speculated on whether Marge's female muscles could provide enough power to propel the boy out of the Earth's atmosphere. Scientists would take notes, publish papers. In reality, Marge would shoot him nasty looks and admonitions: "You better watch your smart mouth" or "Grow up." His father delivered the real beatings, with an executioner's emotional detachment. They lived in Sundown, in western Canada. Their front room served as Marge's Market, and their garage functioned as an appliance-repair business. They were a family of four: Reg, his father, Marge and Reg's half-sister Paula. After marrying, Reg's parents bought the house and converted its garage into an appliance-repair business. Their son should have grown up with his father's manual dexterity, keen technical mind and physical stamina. But no; he couldn't figure out any of it.

. . .

His mother had died during his infancy. "I have a headache," she'd told her husband, and expired that evening from some neurological condition. Within months of becoming a widower, the man married Marge, who supervised the conversion of their front room into Marge's Market. She redecorated the house to suit her own tastes and cleared away everything that might have reminded anyone of the dead woman. Reg, unable to remember life before Marge, imagined his parents' brief time together, felt free to invent them for himself. Occasionally he needed additional pieces for the jigsaw puzzle in his head and asked Marge about his biological mother. Marge liked death the way other people liked sports or movies; she enjoyed dwelling on those who had died, the lifeless pallor of their skin, how they faced the inevitable with breathless terror.

"Your biological mother"—Marge nearly rolled her eyes as she told him what he already knew—"died of a headache." As if someone who'd died in such a foolish way deserved to be laughed at. His father spent most of his time in the garage, repairing everything people brought him. Sundowners liked to keep their old things fixed instead of buying new ones, as if, by acquiring a new appliance, they were letting a stranger move in. The repairman charged relatively little; his customers promised to pay him in barter—"If there's anything I can do..."—knowing he didn't much want or need anything from them. He considered his finances a private matter, and when Revenue Canada audited him posthumously, Marge had to go out to the garage and sort through his three-ring binders bursting with debris accumulated over the years—papers, slips, tattered manila envelopes. Often the papers contained bits of wisdom: *Computers will rule the world someday. Be here now—Ram Dass. June 6, D-Day. "The road of excess leads to the palace of wisdom," Blake.*

Marge was puzzled, anxious. She asked Reg, Who is Ram Dass? Is he a Paki who owes us money? Reg knew but said he didn't. A teenager by then, he decided he'd already learned more than he wanted to know. When the six o'clock news came on, he ran and hid. The garage smelled of grease and sweat. One whole wall glittered with tools hanging from hooks and nails. The repairman, a chain-smoker, had pilfered Player's Lights from Marge's Market and his cough sounded like a saw ripping through wood. Reg wondered why his father smoked when it made him cough like that, but Sundowners considered smoking harmless back then. In the summer, some men sat on benches and coughed most of the time from the "workingman's disease," although Reg couldn't picture any of them ever working. The men just sat on the bench outside Marge's Market and insulted passersby with wolf whistles and chuckles.

Noise came from the garage sometimes. Men argued and got enraged, ready to fight. Often a woman joined in. These agitated voices came from the portable Sony sitting on one of the higher shelves. Reg's father listened to the Bayporte talk station.

"Politicians are scumbags!" he shouted at the radio. "Hang em by their balls!" He called the Vietnam War a criminal act. Reg stood in the distance, unseen, frowning.

Many years earlier, men had carved Sundown out of the forest surrounding the huge, treacherous Jessop River. Then they started making the next town, Brandiz, and mostly forgot about Sundown, which became a town of cracked sidewalks and feeble streetlights. Reg, liked to picture himself on a skateboard, zooming through the streets, in baggy jeans and an oversized T-shirt, daring and dangerous.

Reg and Marge tolerated each other well, at least at first. Before reaching school age, Reg spent entire days in the store with Marge. Paula, a pink warm lump of sleeping flesh, lay by the large front window, as if for sale along with the Pampers and Gerbers.

Marge's Market did a good business with Sundowners who came in out of boredom. Farmers and other country people would tell Marge about bears or wolves they had just seen checking things out at the edge of town, but most of the bigger animals knew better than to come close and be shot at. A handful of people always strolled in and out of the town's stores. One of them was Pearl Stimmel.

Pearl, without asking permission, hoisted herself onto Marge's counter and pushed aside whatever got in her way. She looked down at a tray containing cream-filled doughnuts and asked, "These things fresh?" Then she picked up one and started nibbling at it. "I need a friend, Margie. Someone I can talk to. Will *you* be my friend?"

"You could go talk to Don. He seems like a decent enough fellow."

"Talk to Donna? Get real." Her brother, Don, a timid, girlish bachelor, practiced law. Pearl laughed, a wild manic roar that a zoo creature might make.

A white-faced, crippled monkey-woman not much bigger than a child, Pearl limped along in leather slacks and little black boots. She kept her hair in a tangled but tidy do and her eyes were always scanning the room. Reg feared her bulky sweaters, rouged cheeks and infernal laugh. He knew she had been hospitalized in Bayporte as a child, where a hotshot orthopedic surgeon tried to fix her up. But the operation obviously hadn't worked completely, and Reg wondered: Why hadn't the old crone just stayed in Bayporte, a big city that was full of places for people like her? (He hated to think that there *were* other people like Pearl Stimmel.)

'Pearl's not crazy or stupid,' Marge had said. 'She's as mentally together as the next person. And maybe that's the problem: the little bitch knows she can get away with murder.'

"Hey!" Pearl snapped her fingers at Reg, who had been cowering near the canned goods. "Did your mum ever tell you that I used to live here in Sundown?"

"No," Reg replied.

"Tell the kid it's true, Marge."

"It's true, kid."

"We lived here when Sundown was still worth living in," Pearl said. "Now, I wouldn't live here for nothing."

"Why did you move away?" Marge asked.

"Because," Pearl said, still nibbling at the doughnut, "Sundown sucks. The newspapers and TV are always going on about 'Jessop Valley economic prosperity'! Hah! Where is it?" She stuffed the entire doughnut into her mouth and chewed it for minutes, her lips foaming up like a rabid dog's.

Marge knew all about the Stimmels. Pearl's old house, a big brick box, long abandoned and slowly imploding, squatted in an isolated section of Sundown. Its roof had partly caved in; its windows were bashed in; appliances hulked in the front yard. The local boys, eager to make some sort of clubhouse of it, dared each other to enter it. They all feared what, or who, might be inside.

Pearl's father, Harry, had practiced law in Sundown for decades. A white-haired soft-spoken old Jew who kept the first dollar he ever made, Marge told Reg. "He was a gentleman to his clients and an S.O.B. to everyone else."

After Pearl came back home from surgery in Bayporte, Harry locked her inside all the time so that people wouldn't laugh at her. Pearl said so to the reporters later on. By then, only Pearl and Don remained. People asked, 'Is Pearl all right?'

'Yes, she is,' said Don.

'Is she putting all this behind her?'

'I believe she already has.'

People believed that Harry Stimmel beat his wife and children. People told each other that Harry had caused Pearl's physical deformity; some thought she was pregnant by her father and had gone to Bayporte for an abortion. Or that Pearl's child had been born, as deformed as its mother, and put up for adoption or just buried somewhere in the nearby mountains.

"Probably just nonsense," said Marge, sighing. She loved gossip and wanted to believe the worst about everyone. The ordinary truth always disappointed her.

"But I guess I've said enough about *that* ugliness."

Actually, she was just getting started.

Here is what happened: three local men, Wilbur Stark, Glenn Lavery and Jimmy Chung, had been paid to go to Harry Stimmel's house at night and rough him up. When they demanded to see him, he came out and stood before them in his pajamas and robe. As snowflakes swirled about them, they told him about the accusations of domestic abuse. They asked

Harry, since he practiced a law, how *he* would punish someone like himself. He told them he felt tired and wanted to go back to bed. Then, as Pearl and Don stood watching from their living room window, the three goons beat Harry until the snow at his feet turned maroon. Then they fled. Harry somehow managed to make it back up to his bedroom to get his car keys. He climbed into his Mercedes and drove all the way to downtown Bayporte. He parked his car, got out and dropped dead.

The bad guys went to prison, but the powerful men who'd put them up to it ensured their prompt release and got them union jobs. Pearl and Don seemed indifferent to it all. They inherited their father's money and bought a house in Brandiz.

Don went to law school and took over their father's practice. Pearl in time got all costumed up and began making her rounds in town. She refused to answer questions about her father's murder and its aftermath.

End of story. Marge waved her hand in front of her face, as if dispelling a pungent fart.

Tragic, she called it.

Marge, in her early thirties, wore the same outfit every day: white sleeveless blouse, black slacks, white running shoes. She meant to show everyone that she was the boss, businesslike, efficient, someone to take seriously. She eschewed makeup, perfume and hair coloring. She kept her dark hair straight and just above the shoulders. Tall and lanky, she had a narrow neck and bony hands. A white, compact face with a smattering of freckles across the bridge of her nose. If she'd had the time and money, she might have cultivated the emaciated, dramatic attractiveness of an aging fashion model; Reg thought this of her much later on. But, in prettying herself up, she would have had to concede that she was doing it for others, too, caring about what they thought of her.

Reg grew up thinking of Marge in contrasts: hard and soft, true and false. Young and old, smart and dumb. She hummed obscure songs and made grim pronouncements about life that flew past his head like ominous clouds. He knew she had worked as a ticket clerk in the TransCanada Railway station near Bayporte's impoverished Lower East End. After work, she and her girlfriends went out for beers and rowdy good conversation. Strong and bold, she feared no rapists, pitied no winos. At some point, sick of city life, she married Reg's father, moved to Sundown and began her new life.

...

"I'll drive you to the moon." Where had *that* come from?

Imagine a sunny springtime day, when the fog

dissipated just after dawn and the sky remained clear all during the afternoon, with the promise (or threat) of summer heat just beginning to simmer. The Jessop River took on a new sheen and birdcalls became louder. Sometimes Marge, restless and energized, left Reg in charge of the store while she went over the bridge to Brandiz for shopping and socializing. There she met the mayor's wife, the doctor's wife, the preacher's wife. They talked and she listened; over dinner at home, she made her kids squeal with cruel imitations of those women. Towards the end of her day she would go into the Valley Inn for dessert. The inn had exotic treats, and Reg always asked what she ordered. He smiled if she said Baked Alaska, frowned if she told him apple pie or a banana split. Afterwards she would sit on a bench outside, marveling at the beauty of Brandiz, and smoke an Export A. Her store made most of its profits off cigarette sales and she smoked Export A's because they didn't sell as well as the others. Marge would have hated smokers if she hadn't been one herself.

He's happy when she's happy. He knows that if she's angry, it's usually about money. Maybe deadbeats are late with his payments, or her creditors are getting nasty. Maybe it's one of those things he doesn't understand, like she's getting nostalgic for her younger, freer days.

Once, on the Brandiz side of the bridge, she saw an adolescent male peering over the side, as if he'd dropped something into the Jessop River. Pallid, emaciated, alienated small-town boy. Was he suicidal? As she passed by him and chose not to ask, he reached to his sides and pulled down his jeans. He must have suffered horribly on that day, an afternoon so cold that Marge's jaw vibrated from the relentless, icy wind.

When she first realized what he was doing, and what she was seeing, all she could think was, *Why isn't that boy wearing thermal underpants?*

She meant it in all seriousness, like a concerned

mother. Marge despised profanity; she would tell people to watch their "potty mouths" or take their filth elsewhere.

So: on this Saturday, Marge decides to stay home and do some of the "hundred things" she's always procrastinating on. Reg can't understand her foul mood, wonders if it's one of those mysterious tangles with Reg have already begun, they started years earlier, when he was an infant and she a new bride who didn't know a cotton-swaddled baby could be such a tiny terror, screaming and spitting till it got its own way. They are moving furniture and other items to make space; Marge wants to scrub and polish. Paula, still small, does what little she can.

"You," Marge says to Reg. One can nearly see scripts in their hands, microphones at their chins, a studio audience ready to laugh at their tomfoolery. "You're such a bad influence on your sister."

"Me?"

"She just repeats whatever you say to her." Marge then goes looking for something on the other side of the room.

"Casey Jones," Reg murmurs as Marge busies herself. A minute later, Marge comes back, then drifts away to do something else. Paula looks at one, then the other. Reg repeats, a bit louder, "Casey Jones—"

"Was a son of a bitch!" Paula squeals.

That is what so enrages Marge.

Reg has known that little rhyme for years, and it interests him far more than Canadian history or French nouns. He went home one day and said to Marge, "Who was Casey Jones?"

"I've never heard of her."

"Casey Jones was a he, not a she. But who *was* he?"

"Did you learn about him at school? What did the teacher say?"

Reg smiled, finally reaching the moment when, at Marge's insistence, he would have to say it aloud.

"Casey Jones was a son of a bitch/Drove his train in a thirty-foot ditch."

"Ohhhhh!" Marge threw back her head, as if struck by a heart attack. "Don't you *ever* say anything like that again!"

Reg muttered the lines to himself, weighing them against each other, isolating individual words and then dicing them into syllables. He mostly got a special sense of gratification from picturing Casey Jones himself, randy old fellow, climbing out of that ditch and eager to tell how he got there.

Recently at school they've been talking about Casey Jones again. Reg has brought it home to Paula, who is pleased to have something to share with her older brother.

"Hey!" Marge snaps. "No more of that talk. You hear me?"

Paula hears. She scampers out the back door, to the myriad amusements she's discovered in her brief life.

As a girl, and therefore considered useless, Paula is free to do as she pleases. She does not participate in the household's politics and has no voice in family matters. If this child were made of Styrofoam, Reg and Marge would use her to whack each other over the head.

Marge says it's time to scrub the floor, so she gets out the equipment—pail, brush, rags. Reg sits on the counter while she works, his bottom encased in denim shorts so faded and rented that even he realizes he should be embarrassed by them.

Marge, on all fours, cleans away the filth that has invaded her home: scrub, wipe, scrub, wipe. Her pale limbs are long and sinewy, her muscles popping like an athlete's. She does this work with a hard-breathing violence, as if personally affronted by the filth.

Why do these two fight so often? It is irrelevant by now. Marge objects to his discourtesy, sloth and arrogance. His eagerness to avoid work someone else might end up doing. She speaks of Paula's innocence, Reg's decadence. Everything's just a bloody joke to you, she says, and adds, What's the story with you, anyway? What's your problem? Reg shakes his head, infuriating her with his muteness. He opens his mouth to explain himself, but she holds up her hand to silence him. She grinds her teeth in rage; doesn't she know that he's just provoking her? She becomes animated, waving her arms, staring at his face and accusing him of stealing her life, saying it as if he'd lifted her wallet or made off with her car.

She met a young widower with his baby son and thought, How will they get by without my help? So she married this man and gave him a daughter, and what does she get? A filthy floor and a stepson full of backtalk.

They hear the door open; a customer enters. They're in the middle of a battle, their worst fight—their best one--in months. Marge looks in the direction of the door with the annoyance of a lover receiving a crucial phone call while in the throes of passion. Still, she goes in and welcomes the person who has interrupted her.

"Workin hard or hardly workin, Marge?"

Marge, adept at making sure that a ten-second conversation doesn't go on for eleven, rings up her customer's purchase and sends him away.

"You're so selfish, I can't believe it," she says to Reg a minute later. "Do you ever consider how your actions might affect others?"

"I've never meant to cause you any trouble. I'm sorry if I have made things hard for you."

Reg says these things with a born actor's gentle yet passionate insincerity. Marge grabs a solvent-stiffened rag and fires it at him. He catches it easily and twirls it about on his finger.

"I'm through," says Marge. "Now you're going to get yours."

She marches away, throws open the back door and heads over to the garage. She calls out to the repairman as if she were a prison guard yelling to the executioner that a condemned man's time is up. The big man will stop his work immediately and listen to his wife.

The floor is made of garishly colored linoleum scraps Marge bought almost for free and miraculously fashioned into something like abstract art. Reg, sitting like a cross-legged little Buddha, stares at the floor, grooving on those psychedelic colors: sunbursts, heavenly blues, earthy greens. He hears Marge come crunching back, her unmistakable tread taking its time. In this drama, or comedy, or tragedy, the players' script has run out; they need another actor to get things started up again.

Then he hears the heavy footsteps of his father. Reg's limbs go icy; his heart speeds up. The passionate worker is angry about being taken away from the sacred chore of fixing broken things and arguing with his radio.

"What's your *problem*?" the big man asks.

"It's Reg—he's difficult and disrespectful; he won't mind his manners; he just laughs whenever he's asked to help out." Marge answers him in a voice full of exasperation but stopping just short of a whine. She hates having to make such a big deal about this, but if *she* had ever been that cheeky with *her* mother...

Reg shakes his head and says no, she's wrong.

Are you calling me a liar?

Reg says that he didn't mean any offense, he didn't mean to provoke her, he was just standing up for himself. Marge grabs at her back, holding herself up the way a pregnant woman might, while Reg plays with the stiffened rag.

The repairman folds his arms, nodding.

Reg says, "Not true—"

"Shut it." The big man doesn't look at him.

"Let's keep our dirty laundry to ourselves." Marge

walks across the floor and locks the front door of the store. "This kid mocks me. He laughs at me. He thinks I'm an idiot."

"No!" says Reg.

His father lifts a hand to warn him.

"I need to get your father involved because you won't obey me," Marge says to Reg. "You refuse to take me seriously."

"I've heard enough." The big man loosens his belt. Reg and Marge exchange fearful, even horrified looks, as if the doctor were entering the execution chamber to end a convict's life.

"Maybe there's some alternative to this." Marge's eyes darting around the room as if she's the lawyer who can use the phone to get a stay of execution. Or maybe there's some doorway or nook she and the doomed guy can disappear into.

The man doesn't answer. He knows that the person he is about to exterminate has had more lawyers and days in court than most people get in a lifetime. He walks up to Reg and stares down at his son's bloodless face. He's Doctor Death now, the role with which he is least familiar as a parent. Usually he hides out in his garage with his lame appliances and lets Marge discipline the boy. But this time he must do it, as if he were a surgeon with a scalpel. I'll have to mutilate you in order to save you.

Reg looks around the kitchen, at the furniture he has known for so long and considered his inanimate friends. But they are of no use to him now; even the crazy multicolored linoleum can provide no comfort.

"Oh, don't use the belt," Marge says. "The belt isn't really necessary."

He doesn't reply, which is his way of replying, Be quiet. He walks over and shoves his son off the counter. Reg thinks of them all as actors now, scripts in hand. Maybe this big man is dyslexic and can't read his script, but he knows his part, if not his lines, so he does what is needed to advance the plot.

"Drop your pants!"

Reg does as told, his limbs so stiff with terror that he feels frozen.

Whack!

Feeling the first sting, he hitches up his shorts and darts about the room. Once they're fastened, he becomes more mobile but can't dart from the burly man with his leather bludgeon.

"Sissy! Coward!" The man soon drops the belt and backhands his boy to the ears, face, chest. Reg feels for a moment like a prizefighter he saw on TV, tied up on the ropes, being pummeled no matter which way he bobs or weaves.

He hears himself scream, *Please! No more!*

Marge is screaming too, her voice like a high-pitched wind in Reg's ears. *Stop! Enough!*

Not yet. The man runs Reg across the room like a wrestler wanting to brain an opponent against a blunt object. Then he lets go and the boy crumples to the floor. The man lands a succession of kicks and Reg, curling up like a hound, cups his hands over his gonads. He's not saying anything now, just making noises of distress. Marge grabs at the air, like a mime pulling away an imaginary brute. *Stop! The neighbors will call the cops!*

He's not quite done. His kicks were mostly fakes, his backhands mostly fingers. Reg can tell he has no bruises; he is humiliated but uninjured. Really, has his father ever hurt him in a way that lasted more than an hour? He almost wishes such a beating would happen, so that he could go to school with the scars of parental abuse, be called into the office, watch Marge and his father try to explain things away.

The man falters, wheezes; his belly heaves. Reaching into his back pocket, he pulls out a handkerchief and mops his sweaty brow.

Reg scoots away, Marge throws open the door and shoves him towards the stairs like an emergency worker rushing someone from a disaster site.

"Get up there now! Fast as you can!"

Taking the stairs two at a time, nearly tripping, Reg scampers into his bedroom and eases his door shut, then curls up on his bed, hearing only his heartbeat. Concentrating, he can hear the voices downstairs and can guess what they're saying.

You shouldn't have been so hard on him. He's just a kid and you're a big man.

You're the one always sayin I'm too easy with him, now you're sayin I was too hard. Crazy woman.

I didn't want you giving him a licking that bad.

Their drama continues. Marge, more confident, sounds righteously indignant. Soon she is into one of her monologues and her husband says nothing. Reg thinks the man just wants to go back to his power tools, broken appliances and radio fights.

At times Reg's difficult world seems perfectly controllable. He resolves never to speak to them again, to fill them with remorse over their abysmal mistreatment of him. He feels like one of the *Peanuts* kids he's seen in those Charlie Brown TV specials, the pint-sized bosses who run the world; adults are never seen and speak only through queer wah-wah sound effects. Reg will run things from now on. He will punish those grown-ups, finish them off, do them in.

What if he were to die now? What if he committed suicide, or ran away from home and his body, bloated and bluish, was fished out of the mighty Tyson River weeks later? His options are all equally desirable. These possibilities float about in the ether of his mind; he smirks at a merciless universe suddenly rendered irrelevant.

But soon he feels his omnipotence dissolve, as if he were savoring a forbidden movie viewed in darkened silence, spoiled by a light turned on by an unexpected, harsh adult. The movie continues, but the fun is over.

Reg hears Marge come up the stairs, but he's not ready to accept whatever she has in mind to offer. Still, she gives his door the tiniest tap before entering with a shiny white tube of something.

"Hey there. I don't think he really means to hurt you. Use some of this if you need it."

Reg, face down, half-opens an eye towards his stepmother but says nothing. After a few moments of silence, Marge sighs. "O.K. If you need anything, I'll be downstairs."

As a goodwill gesture, she leaves something at his

door: a cellophane package containing salmon spread and crackers; barbecue chips; a can of Coca-Cola and a Hershey bar. Reg could not have asked for a finer plate of goodies, but at first will refuse to eat any of it, if only to make Marge feel badly. He thinks for a moment or so about suicide, starvation and suffocation, but that only makes him hungrier, so he rips the salmon and crackers out of the flimsy packaging, gobbles it all down and starts in on the barbecue chips and candy bar. He mutters profanities, at himself and the two bullies downstairs, and feels a bit disgusted at the warm, satisfying sensation in his stomach. He will punish them, get back at them, next time.

Marge will come up for the debris-strewn tray and remain silent, for what is there for her to say? They have all forgiven each other. They will remain a family, eating, sleeping, working, fighting, until they separate, through marriage or death or simple restlessness. Reg will enjoy his parents' quiet remorse until time and everyday demands render their conflict meaningless, and when this matter is essentially forgotten about, he will subtly begin provoking Marge again.

On one evening much like this one, in the late spring or summer, a couple of old men had spent hours on the bench outside Marge's Market.

"You know what those coots were sayin?" asked Reg's father.

"No. Do tell," said Marge.

The old coots were convinced that the especially bright star, the first one visible that evening, was actually a CIA-built UFO on its way to the Soviet

Union, to take secret pictures so the Americans could win the Cold War.

"I tried to tell them that the bright light was just another planet."

"Imbeciles," said Marge, who scarcely knew one planet from the others. She still blushed when she learned that Mount Rushmore wasn't a natural rock formation.

To get this conversation away from things she found confusing, she went over to the table where they kept fruit and picked up some oranges. She began juggling them.

Paula shrieked, "I love it!"

Marge, strong and fast, could do expert card tricks and cartwheels. Whenever levity was necessary, she entertained her family.

They watched as she juggled six oranges, her technique flawless and eyes bulging in comic exaggeration. When she finished, they all cheered.

"Bravo! Bravo! A heavenly body!" Reg's father called out, and a genuine feeling of familial contentment settled in the room.

...

A long time later, on a weekend. Reg, living in Bayporte, is flipping through TV channels and ends up watching community-access programs. He sees an ancient, wrinkled Chinese man, his head a hairless, liver-spotted bean. Smiling, being interviewed. Reg turns up the sound.

Yeah, right. World change a lot over the time.

"Would you say it's better or worse now?" asks the interviewer, certainly quite pleased that his subject is in the mood to talk.

No better, no worse. Just different. I hundid years old now.

"Yes, sir. That's a remarkable achievement."

I know.

Reg got up to fix breakfast but kept listening to the program. The old man had a mean little smile and at first Reg thought this might be some sort of malicious parody of old age, with some Asian actor made up to look old. Experimental TV, tasteless, the kind of thing you usually saw on the community channel.

"You worked for many years at Killeen's Brewery. Was it hard work?"

Sometime very hard work. Then better machine, easy work.

"So what's the secret behind making good beer?"

We put a dead Paki in the vat. Make better flavor. Tee-hee.

Oh, so it *was* a real interview, Reg thought. Otherwise they would have deleted that Paki remark. He should have known it was real. No makeup artist could age someone like that.

Brewery work easy. Foundry work hard. Hard and dangerous.

"Did you watch TV or go to the movies? What did you do for fun?"

No watch TV or go to movies. We made our own fun.

Then the announcer said, "That was Mr. James Chung from Sundown on his one hundredth birthday. He died last week, six months after this interview. We visited with him at the Seniors' Center."

Jimmy Chung.

Bully and murderer who lived to be one hundred. Interviewed on his birthday by a TV reporter who knew nothing about the night Chung, Will Wark and Glenn Lavery had roughed up lawyer Harry Stimmel and gone to prison for it. Jimmy Chung, member of the one hundred club, the few and the proud.

Sitting in his living room, Reg wanted to tell someone about Chung's birthday and Harry Stimmel. Marge would have liked that. She had that way of scratching her chin while saying *Tragic* as she savored another's misfortune. She, too, was in the Seniors' Center now, and Reg felt full of anxiety whenever he thought of contacting her. She had been in there, on another floor, when the TV crew arrived to see

Chung, but probably would not have understood any of it. When Reg first put Marge in the Center, she became hostile and mostly mute, sitting in bed with her arms folded, snarling at the nurses and telling them to kiss her ass.

GEORGE ONSTOT

Fortunate Ones

As an adult, Reg met many moderately affluent people who wished they'd had impoverished childhoods to overcome. So he would entertain them with stories about his own hardscrabble Sundown youth. He told them about scandals and squalor, crumbling concrete school outhouses and dope-smoking teachers. He sometimes mentioned siblings Johnnyboy and Dee Dee Rae. Reg really didn't think such stories were quite as funny as everyone else did, but perhaps because Reg made them so funny, people kept laughing, so he told them whenever the subject came up. To him, most of the time, they were like dirty jokes, to be enjoyed for a moment and forgotten The boys' and girls' outhouses had flimsy doors that creaked when swung open, but one couldn't see in from the outside due to a recessed entryway. In the winter, frigid wind blew in, and in the summer, the deteriorating little facilities sweltered. They had been built with modest frosted windows that could be slid open for air. from poorly aimed deposits. Some students relieved themselves next to the toilets.

Reg shuddered in disgust and hurried home, sometimes with his eyes circulation, but boys had shattered them, along with the plywood sheets that replaced those windows. The splintered toilets were discolored watering and bowels screaming. Occasionally he knew he couldn't make it home and hid behind by a tree halfway home, shivering with embarrassment as he fouled himself.

"Dirty dog!" Marge howled when she saw his condition. "Woof, woof!"

Reg knew that she got some satisfaction from such moments because they confirmed that he, her uppity stepson, was just as human as everyone else and what he needed to learn was some humility. He told her very little about the outhouses, knowing she would have arrived at his school some morning, a one-woman cleaning crew, shouting, "If this mess happens again, I'll call the school board and get you all fired!" Reg considered school a mere microcosm of the universe, perplexing and unalterable, indifferent, eternal. He had started collecting moments of outrageousness for a mental scrapbook he would never share with Marge. He would tell others only when enough time had passed for such things to have lost the power to disturb him.

Some Sundowners were fanatically religious. Most were Roman Catholics or fundamentalist Protestants, hating each other because their brash, opinionated parents had taught them to do so. The poorest Christians attended Sally Ann's love-and-brotherhood services and many of the Catholics started each morning in prayer, regardless of what they would do that day or to whom.

"Hypocrites," Marge said. "Catholics will sell you a ticket to heaven no matter what you've done and the Protestants are no bloody better." Reg watched the TV news sometimes. He saw reports from Belfast, young men killing each other to prove that killing was wrong. And what about all the atrocities happening in other parts of the world...?

A cluster of students gathered in red-faced silence and uncontrollable eagerness for the finest show in the Valley, whispered around school by incredulous, delighted children about what was going on in the woods:

"Johnnyboy is diddling Dee Dee!"

Brother diddling sister.

Fornicating, Marge would have said. Copulating, coitus, as if it were a legal matter with courtrooms and lawyers and transcripts. Something requiring a license. Johnnyboy and Dee Dee. How had *that* gotten started? Reg guessed Johnnyboy did it to impress his friends; short and freckled like his sister—after all, they were identical twins—Johnnyboy suffered from a small male's lack of self-assurance and a need to gain approval in whatever way he could. Dee Dee surely did not want to participate in Johnnyboy's fun. They had to catch her first, and she would run away like a terrified puppy that knew something bad awaited it. So the boys outran her, then carried her into the woods. Did she know what they had in mind for her? She certainly knew one thing: that nobody ever seemed to consider *her* feelings. Dee Dee Rae had suffered a severe head injury when someone slammed her head into a wall, according to Marge. Someone else said Dee Dee's father, drunk, had tossed her into the air but forgot to catch her. Another story went that a careless nurse had deprived her of oxygen at birth. Her looks had been spared; she had a pretty, freckled face with pellucid eyes and a sunny blonde smile. At school, she couldn't do more than the simplest reading and writing; her teachers left her alone to doodle and daydream while they concentrated on the students who had shown some potential. She may not have been as stupid as everybody thought, either, but simply shell-shocked, overwhelmed by snickering classmates and exasperated teachers. Still, she usually smiled (although perhaps in terror) and seemed strangely optimistic. She would follow people around if they appeared willing to endure her company and listen as she rambled. You had to walk away from her, or get even tougher than that: Go away, Dee Dee. Get lost or I will smack you silly. I swear to God.

Johnnyboy and his pals didn't use condoms and Dee Dee did not get a tubal ligation. She got pregnant, would get an abortion in Bayporte and get pregnant again. What did you do about a problem like Dee Dee? She solved the problem herself by suddenly dying of an infection one winter. For years afterwards, Reg saw Dee Dees in books and movies in which a pretty, damaged girl or boy was exploited by a manipulative, opportunistic world. But he noticed that they made her seem somehow wanton and corrupted, a blank-faced nymphet with a plunging neckline, secretly inviting the brutal encounters with the local boys.

Dee Dee hated Johnnyboy. While being carried to the edge of the woods, she grunted and screamed, kicked and slapped. Sometimes she lost a shoe or both of them, and maybe her socks, too. At such times she looked too healthy, too able to be the pitiful Dee Dee Rae. Of course, Reg could not see her well, because she was petite and he, like many others, remained at the foot of the woods as the big boys went in for a closer look, or more than just a look. But she was only Dee Dee, a person not precisely regarded as somebody, and the boys and girls soon lost interest and wandered off.

Reg, years later, told people about these things and they laughed in disbelief, saying, "What an awful time you must have had! What a dreadful education!" But Reg had learned about getting along with his peers and staying in one piece when the frustrated Sundown kids vandalized the school once each year. He had tried to be a one-person Switzerland— everybody's friend, or at least nobody's enemy—but soon he had to choose sides. Sundown had no fences to straddle.   He figured he was best off by making friends with those who lived closest to him, so they could walk home together with less chance of being pelted with snowballs or Coke bottles. He could never understand why people fought, whether in Sundown or Palestine. Ignorant of the dirty tricks of street fighting, he was unreliable in a fracas. Reg was generally happy, except when he needed to use the bathroom. Survival in high school, no matter its difficulties and frustrations, was not precisely an ordeal for him. Survival could be fun.

Reg learned to shoo Dee Dee away. He stayed out of the damp, dark, smelly school basement and hurried past the myriad nooks and crannies where the bigger boys were waiting to flick their lit cigarettes at passersby. He made a big mistake one day in telling Marge the truth when a big boy, one of the Doyles, bumped into him and bent his new glasses. Marge went to the school to straighten them out (as she liked to put it). Some of the other students said that Reg had bent them himself. The teacher, poker-faced, wondered what Marge wanted of her. In Sundown, parents stayed away from the school and didn't harass teachers. In the neighborhood, fathers were vocal when their boys were in fights, would shout encouragement, even physically protect a bloodied son. At home they vilified the teacher and instructed their children not to take any of her backtalk. But only Marge would actually *go* to the school and confront the teacher. What did Marge want? An apology from the bully and an offer to pay to have the glasses replaced.

Everyone but Marge seemed to understand that snitching was bad and justice would never be done just because someone's momma showed up. Bent glasses, ripped clothing and stolen property were just parts of school life.

"The teacher is a fool," Marge said.

No, thought Reg, just a lady doing her job. She didn't try to be anyone's surrogate mother or aunt. She locked the classroom door during recess and, outside, the boys could slap each other around as much as they wanted, steal whatever wasn't bolted down, leer at the girls. Sundown boys went to school because there was nothing else for them to do. They were big and strong enough for jobs, but their fathers and uncles had the worthwhile employment. The girls could get domestic jobs once they turned sixteen, so they stayed in school only if they were going on to college. Some of them spoke of moving to Bayporte, as if the big city offered legitimate opportunities to small-town girls. The teacher had a very businesslike manner at school, uninterested in her students' personal lives. She often got their names confused. Although she probably wanted to retire, her husband had lost an arm in a logging accident and they needed income, so she drove in from Brandiz in herold Toyota and taught those who wanted to learn. Many of her students went on to graduate from Northup University. She challenged her students to improve their minds as the pipes groaned, water leaked and snow fell outside. Heaters didn't work or worked too well, the desks grew rickety. But education happened—spelling, grammar, geography. Facts, tables, lessons. The teacher maintained order and guided the students through each day's material.

She smoked pot. She would light up in her car and suck passionately, eyes watering, lips quivering. Reg saw her and would never have guessed that such a skinny, humorless, contemptuous woman had a vice like that. She struck him as the kind of person to call the cops on dopers getting high in the park.

Marge would have said the teacher was dumb to smoke pot. Marijuana and heroin rotted your brain. Cigarettes merely gave you cancer.

One thing in the school impressed everybody as

charming and memorable. The hallways were covered with murals too high to risk defacement. Paintings of boys and girls. Reg didn't know who'd painted them, but they were beautiful. A redheaded boy, a black girl; a Mexican; a Chinaman. The colors clear and long-lasting. Backgrounds of pure snow, of blossoming branches, of heady summer sky. They were bright and eloquent, so dichotomous with everything else that what they seemed to represent was not the kids everywhere, not those skies and snows, but some other world of peace and innocence, mutual respect and dignity.

In those murals, no was ripping off anyone else. Nobody was insulting others; there was no slashed clothing, there were no slapped faces or kicked scrotums. No gangbanging in the nearby woods; no Dee Dee and Johnnyboy Rae.

There were three big boys in Advanced Placement: Kenny, Neal and Adam. They comprised the entire class, and Advanced Placement was to prepare them for Northup. Three kings. But when you looked closer, a king and two princes. That was how Reg perceived them. They sauntered around the schoolyard together, Neal in the middle. He was the tallest. Ken and Adam leaning against and leading up to him.

Reg admired Neal.

Neal lived with his grandparents. His grandmother went across the bridge to Brandiz, to do cleaning and ironing. His grandfather was a plumber.

Neal was illegitimate. His mother worked somewhere or was married. Perhaps she worked as a maid, and sent him send cast-offs, or she shopped carefully at the Sally Ann and sent her son clothing she knew would flatter him. He came to school in double-pleated wool slacks, skinny ties, double-breasted suit jackets. Even when the clothing did not look like the sort of thing someone his age should wear, he could carry it off. His clothes hung on him just right. He was not so much talented as magical, not so much handsome as present. His looks would go hard and mean over time. But for now he was regal, walking in the schoolyard with his attendants.

He did not waste any attention on the girls at school, none of those boys did. They were waiting, perhaps already acquiring, real girlfriends (Neal would have said *women*). Some girls called to them from the basement door, wistfully insulting, and Neal turned and fixed them with a deathly stare until they wilted and hurried away.

Reg had no idea what his stare meant but was full of admiration for the way Neal turned on his hips for the taunting, cruel yet lazy and unperturbed sound of his voice, his glossy look. When alone, Reg would act that out, the whole scene, the girls calling, Reg pretending to be be Neal. He would turn just as Neal did, on those imaginary girls, and just *stare*.

Reg walked around the yard behind the store, imagining himself in Neal's eclectic attire. You could smell him, too. His aftershave lotion.

…

The three of them sat at the top of the fire escape, in the first warm weather. They were smoking cigarettes. Reg had meant to go up the fire escape into the school as he usually did, avoiding the everyday threat of the main entrance, but when he saw those boys he turned back, not expecting them to move to make room for him.

Neal said, "Reg, come on up if you want. Have a smoke."

"Then they'll all want one," said Adam.

"No. Just him." Neal thought for a moment. "Yeah, Reg, just Reg. Come on up."

When Reg reached them, Neal offered him a handshake, then shook out a cigarette from their package and held it out to Reg, whose fingers shook as he accepted it.

"Is Reg your real name?" asked Neal.

"Reginald."

Neal was being diplomatic, talking to him as if they had been friends all their lives. Reg was too dazzled, and too suspicious, to fully enjoy this apparent acceptance from these popular boys. What would they expect from him in return? Did they expect to bum money from him? Did they expect him to help them rob Marge's Market?

Reg was hooked. He wanted to join this clique and studied their movements and behaviors like an actor researching a part. This was how winners looked; what they did was what everyone should do. At school, there was a certain music, an irresistible charm, to everything Neal did or said. He sighed at the mention of a test or grinned at the sound of the three-o'clock bell. Neal had a habit of rubbing his chin with the side of his right fist.

Imitation was not enough. Reg went further. He imagined being sick and Neal would somehow be called to look after him. They could watch TV together. He made up stories of danger and rescue, accidents and gratitude. Sometime he rescued Neal, sometimes Neal rescued Reg. Then all was warmth, indulgence, revelation.

Hey, Reg.

Join us for a smoke.

The opening, the increase, the beginnings of brotherhood. Sexual love and girls were too complicated for Reg; he needed to concentrate on something more comprehensible and attainable. When things were flowering—lilacs, apple trees, hawthorns along the road—the girls had the game of funerals, organized by the older girls, and the boys watched. The person who was supposed to be dead— a girl, only girls played this game but boys, frightened and aroused, watched from a respectful distance—lay stretched out on the top of the fire escape. The rest filed up slowly, singing some hymn, and cast down their armloads of flowers. They bent over pretending to weep (some did more than just pretend) and took the last look. That was all they did. Every girl who wanted to play dead was supposed to get her chance, but as soon as the older girls got theirs, they lost interest. The person playing dead got to choose what the processional hymn would be. They all sounded the same to Reg. The girl playing dead would lay heaped with flowers; she wore her best dress with beads and a brooch. At times the girl, with all this attention, twitched; her eyeballs fluttered. Her expression was serene, tranquil, glad to be done with the nonsense of living.

Reg made a big mistake soon. He stole cigarettes from Marge's store to give to Neal. His mistake was not just in the stealing, though that was stupid and difficult. Marge kept the cigarettes up behind the counter on a slanted shelf in open boxes, out of reach. Reg had to wait for his chance, then reach over and grab the Player's Lights. He didn't smoke them himself. He stuffed the small blue-and-white box into his pocket and wrapped himself with his arms, as if the package were conspicuous. Marge saw how he hugged himself and said, "Why are you doing that? Are you coming down with a cold?" He shook his head and went away.

Reg thought of nothing but the cigarettes and waited for the chance to slip the package into Neal's desk but the chance didn't come along nearly as quickly as he would have expected. Even if he had walked up to Marge or someone else and paid for the cigarettes it would have been inappropriate, in the beginning maybe but not now.

By now, Reg's expectations of Neal in the way of thanks were too high; any gesture would have made Reg feel insulted. His heart thundered in his ears if Neal so much as walked by his desk in his towering way, with his "I shall own the world one day" walk. Reg knew that whatever conversation followed the cigarettes would have made him feel ludicrous.

Reg saw there would be no right time simply to hand his friend the cigarettes, so he resolved to leave them in Neal's desk, but leaving a cigarette package was not unlike leaving a bag of marijuana or a small bottle of liquor. The teacher was always the last one out to prevent vandalism.

The teacher turned her back and Reg slipped the package into Neal's desk and went home, ambivalent about what he had done.   Days later he understood what happened: Neal found the cigarettes, guessed that they were from Reg, whose stepmother sold most of Sundown's cigarettes. Neal took them to Marge, knowing that Reg had no money for cigarettes and had probably stolen them. Neal didn't want to get Reg into trouble with Marge. He didn't want Reg's cigarettes, either, because he could get his own easily enough. What interested Neal was walking into the store and returning the shoplifted goods and in having himself thought of as an honorable young man who did the right things.

"'I'm not sure why he thought it was a good idea, stealing from you to give to me. Does he think he's Robin Hood?'" Marge remembered Neal as saying. Reg did not believe her; Neal wouldn't have condescended to speak to Sundown's humble shopkeeper.

The package of Player's Lights was not in saleable condition now. Its box was warped from having been in Reg's pocket for so long, and a rent ran through its cellophane wrapping. Marge didn't like Player's Lights but didn't want to give away this, expensive item, either. She smoked this ruined package to avoid wasting it.

Marge couldn't believe it. She was too shocked to be angry. The theft itself was awful, of course, but there was another matter that concerned her more.

"Why did you give those cigarettes to him? Are you sweet on him or something?"

She smirked, trying to be an older brother or pal to him. He was supposed to smirk and say, "Oh, fuck off." Marge did that sometimes—tried to speak his language, creep into that vapid fog called male humor.

Reg looked away, his face red.

"That bloody Neal," Marge went on. She shook her head. "Why does everyone look up to him so much? He's more show than substance, I can tell you that. He's not so handsome. Just wait. In a few years, he'll be bald and fat. Where does he get those odd clothes? I guess he thinks they make him look like some kind of Continental gentleman."

Reg said nothing and Marge added that Neal did not have a father, or, rather, that his parents were not married. "Do you know what that makes him? *Do* you?"

Marge could not resist speaking of Neal. She did just that, many times.

"Look! There's your hero!" she would exclaim as she stood in the store, watching Neal walk across the street.

Reg usually just shrugged.

"Oh, you know what I'm talking about. You stole cigarettes from me and gave them to him. You're just too ashamed to admit it."

Reg only partly remembered. He knew the guy's name and face but not the terror and exhilaration. Neal was now a large, paunchy, glowering boy with whiskers. He had a knapsack slung over his shoulder as he trudged along to school. He scarcely read his textbooks and was failing abysmally. He wore denim jackets, sweatshirts and work pants that made him look ungainly. Reg thought that maybe his persona had been shattered because he no longer had fancy attire. He disappeared and joined the Canadian National Forces. He came back for a visit once or twice, looking soft and drab in his uniform. He had married an Asian girl.

Reg was indifferent to Neal's deterioration. Everyone around him, and himself, had undergone some sort of metamorphosis, and some of those changes seemed unfortunate. He thought Marge had been foolish, to retell the story of the cigarettes and making Neal look worse and worse. Reg never saw any sort of lesson in what Marge was saying, and he mostly dismissed her as a jealous, aging, friendless woman.

Beer and Toilet Paper

Reg finished elementary school and started classes at Sundown Secondary. Its rooms were big and still smelled of paint. He had to take Boys' Foods, a progressive course the school dreamed up. Some of the parents didn't like it because it seemed pointless and insulting to make the boys learn girls' stuff. The instructor just wanted to make sure that the boys understood the basics of nutrition. She was chic and young, wearing a blue jacket, matching skirt and white high heels, as if teaching M.B.A. students instead of high school boys. She paced the room, asking questions. "What are some of the major health disorders today?"

An easy question, covered the previous year.

"Diabetes."

"Cancer."

"Heart attacks."

"Strokes."

The teacher made faces, as if the words themselves were diseases. These students were the kids from the right side of the river, the North Sundowners. Reg was unsure he belonged here, but he sat and paid attention, not entirely sure of how much he was going to enjoy the next months.

The teacher asked, "Well, when you go to the grocery store, what are the two main things you boys buy?"

"Beer and toilet paper," Reg blurted. Everybody laughed. Marge wouldn't have thought he was funny. She had gotten after him all his life for saying such things. But Reg was happy with what he'd said, and the underlying truth of it.

He was walking across the bridge after school when he heard something he was sure was meant to get his attention. He walked more softly and looked around. The bridge, like the river, was long and broad; boys liked to play around there, even though the Tyson River was hazardous and. People had drowned there over the years, swallowed up in its beautiful, merciless depths.

Beer and toilet paper!

He would hear those words many times over the years. He would never be sure who said it, or that he cared, although he would always have to wipe anxious sweat off his brow. We need to be careful of what we say.

He knew that other kids had it worse. Ignominy was a part of high school life, where few secrets were honored and fewer things were forgotten. Reg wasn't the boy who lost the condoms. That was some poor kid who had them in his pocket for some unknown reason. There was a condom dispenser in the boys' bathroom that took your money and kept its condoms. Some students resolved to make an issue of it, to tell the school's administration to fix the machine. No one did.

Someone found the condom, stretched it a bit and put it on display near the picture of the principal. It looked worn, as if it contained someone's fluid. Everybody talked about it that day. The principal swore that someone would be expelled over the matter.

Reg often went home to tell Marge about what happened at school. She enjoyed hearing his account of the condoms. There were others.

Bonnie Picard was a slatternly, dimpled brunette who worked at the lumber yard and lived in with a local family as a housekeeper/babysitter. When they went away, as they often did, she was there by herself. On one of those nights, she had three guests over: Carver Fairley, Simpson Lee and Swine Swinofsky.

"They went there to show themselves a good time," said Marge, her voice soft. Reg's father was upstairs and would be offended by such a story.

Carver Fairley was a vain, handsome boy who acted first and thought later. He told the other boys

85

he would go in first, charm Bonnie into taking on all three of them, it would be no problem. The problem, as it turned out, was that Simpson Lee had already gotten Bonnie to promise to meet him in the basement.

"Who knows what was crawling about in that filthy basement," Marge said. "The kids that age don't think about those things."

Carver entered the house and began looking for Bonnie while she was in the basement with Simpson. Swine knew about all of it and eagerly awaited the confrontation between Carver and Simpson as he heard grunts and groans coming from the basement.

Soon Simpson emerged to look for Carver, to see if Carver knew that a big joke was being played on him. Carver was in the kitchen, eating junk food. He said that Bonnie Picard was nothing but a whore and he wouldn't do it with her if she paid him. He wanted to go home.

By then, Swine had slipped into the basement and was getting it on with Bonnie.

"Just imagine!" said Marge.

Simpson then started walking around. Swine and Bonnie, in the dark basement, stopped what they were doing for a moment.

"Who the fuck is that?" asked Bonnie.

"Don't mind him. It's only Simpson."

"What? I thought *you* were Simpson!"

Just imagine!

Reg knew what happened then: Bonnie plunked

down onto the sofa and, after several moments of disgusted staring, said, "I don't like to be treated like the town pump."

"You reap what you sow," said Marge. Reg's father came downstairs, coughing loudly. He had been coughing like that for years, but now he sounded even worse. He sat and coughed some more until he stopped. Then he breathed, deeply and quietly.

"The doc writes him prescription after prescription, but nothing ever seems to help," Marge said. "The quack just sells us the most expensive drugs there are, then says, 'If there's no improvement, come back and see me.'"

"Don't ever let me catch you bringing home anyone like Bonnie," Marge added. "I wouldn't have any of it."

"Not me," Reg said. "I know better."

"Good," Marge said.

. . .

Here is another story that Marge told Reg: When her parents died, she went to live with moderately wealthy aunt who owned a farm. The idea was for Marge to go to school, work occasionally on the farm and, when her education was complete, move away and no longer be a burden on her aunt.

"But they thought education was a frivolous matter that made people uppity and kept their bodies soft. They rarely sent me to school; they kept me busy on the farm."

Her aunt hated the sun and spent most of her

time in the shade. She liked to think she was a character straight out of *Gone with the Wind* and would snap at people over the slightest infraction.

"But she was a pretty woman, and smart, too, so I really couldn't blame her for being the way she was," Marge said.

Part of Marge's job was to deliver the men's dinners to them as they worked. One man opened his dinner and said, "How come there's no cake?"

"Don't ask me, I'm no baker," retorted Marge. It was probably the first time a female had ever spoken to him that way.

He took her back to her aunt and told her what Marge had said. He was a big, aggressive man who would not tolerate disrespectful behavior. The aunt nodded, apologized and gave him a big slice of cake.

He went back to work in the field. Then the aunt hit Marge so hard that her ears rang for a couple of days afterwards. Her school days soon ended. In her early teens she ran away and ended up getting a job at a lumber mill in Sundown But her aunt tracked her down and visited her. You're always welcome to come back, Margie, for a day or a decade. Just remember that. The lumber yard is no place for a proper girl like you. You can go back to school if you want.

So Marge said yes, and when she returned, she ended up doing the most menial canning and cooking work she could imagine. She didn't go to school or become a proper lady; she kept asking herself, Why do I put up with this?

She put up with it, as she later concluded, because she felt sorry for those people.

When her aunt lay dying in the hospital, Marge was on another floor, recovering from a tonsillectomy. Her aunt wanted to see Marge, so Marge agreed to let herself be walked over. When she saw the lady, once full of life and now a long, pallid, lifeless thing stretched across the length of the bed, Marge suffered a panic attack, the only one she would ever have.

"I thought I was the one who was dying. Was I having a stroke, a heart attack? My heart was just pounding. I didn't wait around to say hello or goodbye to her. I just said, 'Get me out of here.'"

"So you didn't get the chance to say goodbye to her," Reg said.

"No, I didn't."

Reg brought home an armload of books every night. Foreign languages, military history, metaphysics. Marge sneered at them all, especially the ones big enough to be doorstops. She flipped through a couple of them, tried to mouth some of the words she encountered, gave up and pushed them aside.

"Why are you reading all this crap?"

His father ambled into the kitchen in his bathrobe. He was retired, or at least too sick and old to work. Reg did not look at him directly and was still fairly sure that his father considered him useless. The books sat there, so that Reg could tacitly say, See these? I am good for something.

"You're learnin to be a real bossypants, eh?" his father said.

Marge smiled. He often tried to amuse her, to stay

on her good side. Reg didn't say anything. He became uncomfortable and wanted to leave the room because he felt that his father was ashamed of him for being a bossypants who read books and talked to people.

Reg knew that his father saw Marge as a noble wife and mother: disciplined, motivated, tough, tender, practical, detailed and lists, and good at calling people out and putting them in their places.

"Women are weird." The man maybe forgot that Reg would soon be in search of a woman to marry. "Don't try to understand them. You never will. But if you accept them for who they are and don't try to make them into something they're not, you'll get more good than bad from them."

Reg decided was the wrong kind of man for women: he spaced out, showed off and wanted to be noticed and complimented. Sundown women wanted men with strong hands and deep pockets. Reg saw his father's disgust and despair whenever anyone suggested that his boy help him at work.

Reg had learned all of this long ago and could easily see himself as his father saw him, so he simply lost himself in books and become engrossed in someone else's thoughts.

Anita Feist, one of Reg's cousins, was over a decade his senior. She lived in an apartment on the edge of Sundown and worked at an auto supply store. After years of conscientious saving, she had bought a new Ford pickup truck. When she visited Marge, Anita stared lovingly out the window at her truck, as if she had won it on a TV game show and still couldn't believe it was hers.

Marge said that Anita was the happiest person she had ever met. "Anita's truck has lots of room. She can make your father comfortable."

"Marge, come up here!" At first, the sick man didn't want to impose on her. But after a while, he called her up just because he was lonely.

"I don't know how he'll get along without me in the hospital," Marge said. "He's getting more dependent each day."

Reg couldn't tell if she was complaining or bragging. Sometimes she would wait until he sounded more desperate, or she would call back, "What do you want, exactly?"

While minding Marge's Market, she told everyone about how often she changed her husband's perspiration-soaked sheets; pinching her nose, she went "Whoo-wee!" Reg hated her for thinking this was funny.

Reg remained in the store, and sometimes he was the only person there. On an overcast, blustery day, he was glad to be indoors. Marge

was getting his father ready for the hospital. Reg thumbed through a tattered copy of *The New Yorker* and found a John Updike story populated by rich, unhappy people somewhere in Massachusetts, surviving life in 1950s America. Everyone in those stories drank bourbon, smoked cigarettes and feared death. Where in Updike's world, Reg wanted to know, were the Sundowners? The poor, rural people who had to launder old men's bedsheets?

Reg heard Anita Feist bound up the couple of stairs and holler, "Long time, no see, eh? Well, here I am."

John Updike's characters did not speak like Anita Feist.

Reg finished the story and imagined having been created by Updike. He would wear an overcoat, smoke cigarettes and speak in a charming New England accent. Updike's people knew everything worth knowing and didn't finish their sentences with "eh?"

"I walked over," Anita said, appearing in the store. "I had to take my boy in, cause he was actin up." Her "boy" was her oversized Ford. "No sense in goin all the way into Bayporte and havin him break down on me, eh?"

Reg had liked Anita Feist ever since he was a child because she had big breasts and would give him a dollar once in a while. "This is for

when you get a girlfriend," she would say.

"So, Reg, what's new? Been mindin your manners?" Anita asked now.

"I suppose."

"I hear you're makin good grades at school. Gonna be a rocket scientist or somethin?" she asked.

He had no interest in rocket science, but people respected you a little bit more when they thought you had such lofty goals. Especially when those people didn't know what a rocket scientist *was*.

"It's just too bad," she said.

"What?"

"About your daddy. Gettin ill, havin to go to the

hospital. It'll happen to all of us one day, I guess."

"He's not dead yet, Anita."

"Didn't say he was. In fact, the doctors down in Bayporte are so good that they'll have him up and dancin soon enough."

"Not if he's as sick as they say." The doctors hadn't said *anything*, yet.

"Oh? What did they say?" Anita asked.

"I would rather not say."

"Come on. I'm family, after all."

Anita phoned the mechanic and found out that her truck wouldn't be ready until later that day. She didn't want to wait all that time, then drive down to Bayporte late at night. She would stay the night on Reg's sofa and take the old man in the morning.

"That's just fine, Anita," said Marge. "I'm sure we'll make it till morning." She and Anita kept gabbling to each other as Reg sat and stared at the cover of *The New Yorker,* wishing he could dive into its pages and explore that huge, fascinating city.

At around dinnertime, Marge closed the store. Reg's father came down. He was dressed presentably, as if for church.

"For such a sick man," Marge said, "you look pretty good. Do you feel good?"

"Same as I always feel," he said. "Maybe the thing I need is to spend less time in bed."

"There you go!" said Anita Feist. "More activity is the way to get feelin better."

Anita had brought over a bottle of Canadian Mist.

She sipped at a glass she'd poured for herself.

"Mind if I have a little glass of that?" Reg asked.

"You got some I.D.?" Anita asked.

"If we give you some," Marge said, "your sister will want some, too, and I don't want her having any."

"What I don't understand," Anita said, "is that there are more docs and hospitals and what-not than ever before, yet there's more illness, too. More sick people than ever before."

"People are living longer," Reg said. "If you live long enough, something will eventually get you."

"Too many patients, not enough docs," said Reg's father. "Whole generation is gettin old, gonna be a burden on the young ones."

"Well, *you're* not a burden on anyone," said Marge.

"Of course I am," said her husband. "But not for much longer."

. . .

Reg walked through the hallways of the new Sundown High School during its week of celebration. It was just a coincidence that he was there; he had come back from Bayporte to check on Marge.

A few people said, "I saw you on TV a few times, Reg. You're coming up in the world, eh?"

The new high school had more of everything and was much bigger.

New gymnasium, cafeteria, classrooms. The condom dispenser always worked.

Carver Fairley owned a gas station.

Simpson Lee had become a tax attorney.

Swine Swinovsky made money in the minerals market. Then he sold his company and used some of the money to run for premier of Great Elizabeth. On TV he alienated his country by saying that Canada just needed to revoke the Canadian citizenship of all those troublemaking Frenchies in Quebec.

The Son and the Moonie

Marge warned Reg about the Chicken Hawks. She said they were in all the big cities, adults looking for boys to exploit. They offered you smiles and kindness, bought you a meal, invited you to spend the night in their guest room. Then they drugged you and shipped you off, across the country or overseas. You ended up in dirty movies bought by goofy old men, and when you got too old for that, they turned you out on the street. Marge said she had learned about Chicken Hawks in Bayporte, when she worked as a ticket clerk in the TransCanada Railway station, which doubled as the city's bus station. She saw them come in, the poor dears, wayward young males——runaways and throwaways from broken homes. They would get off the bus and loiter in the lobby, lost and lonely. They all looked alike: denim jackets, sleeveless T-shirts, meager possessions stuffed into knapsacks slung over their shoulders. After buying a Coke from the lobby machine, they would sit on one of the benches and stare at the vast, handsomely restored old lobby. Then the Chicken Hawk would swoop in, masquerading as a priest, social worker or other do-gooder. Following a few minutes of harmless conversation, the two would disappear through the gigantic front doors.

"I must've seen that happen a zillion times," Marge said.

Reg asked how to tell Chicken Hawks from Good

Samaritans. Marge said she'd worked in the ticket booth till midnight and she just *knew*. "All the perverts came out during my watch." She saw one man knock out the teeth of another man; the victim, blind drunk, didn't seem to feel it. He just stared at the other guy, as if asking, *Hey! Did you just punch me?*

Another time, Marge discovered a dead woman, her face as blue as the afternoon sky, sitting on a ladies' room toilet.

"Well," said Reg, "if *I* had trouble, I would just go to the cops."

Marge hooted. "The cops! They're worse than the criminals!"

Reg didn't think Marge knew everything about human behavior. Father Charles was a good example.

A tall, spare man, he came into Marge's Market sometimes and bought lots of candy. "You look like you could use a day off," he might say to Marge.

"All work and no play..." he would remark if Reg was there. "A boy should be outside, playing football."

After he left, she would go the window and look at Father Charles. "He drives a purple Cadillac. He's up to no good." Marge clucked her tongue. Father Charles, a retired priest, usually wore a suit; Reg couldn't recall ever seeing him in his collar. Marge claimed he drove all over the Valley, looking like a pimp in his Cadillac, using all that candy he bought to get boys into his car. Reg didn't see how it could be; he thought the old man munched on the candy as he drove. "I know better than you do," Marge said. "I know about things." She told Reg the man drove around in the hot weather, singing hymns with the windows rolled down, and what kind of normal man did *that?*

Reg believed Father Charles was just doing what he had done as a priest, calling on the community, checking in on people, doing what good he could.

"Some people are naïve," Marge said. "They believe his lies. They're just asking to be taken advantage of."

Reg shrugged. Guilty until proven innocent, according to Marge.

Reg was taking the train to Bayporte, going alone for the first time. He had made that trip a few times with Marge. When he was small, she said it might be fun for them to and buy their food from the snack bar and eat on board the train. She got him his favorite, a salmon sandwich in a cellophane package. The bread was stale, but he kept nibbling at it, afraid that Marge would notice and make a scene. She did. She plucked the sandwich from his hand and squeezed it with a snarl, as if holding something vile just raked up from the sewer. She marched back to the snack bar and urged the attendant to taste it for himself, then extended the same invitation to the other passengers in line. He offered her another sandwich that was slightly fresher.

"You have to stand up for yourself," Marge said to the onlookers. "You can't let people push you around." Reg gobbled up the new sandwich, but it sat in his stomach like clay, and at first he feared he would vomit. His can of 7-Up was lukewarm. For Reg's first trip alone, Marge escorted him onto the train, and he half expected her to ask some of his fellow passengers to look after him. Once Marge left the train, Reg stretched out across both seats and nearly wept with joy. He reminded himself of the items he needed to find in Bayporte. A special kind of ointment for Marge, and cough drops of a certain brand for his father. A cribbage board, a deck of playing cards.

He wanted a copy of *Playboy* magazine (if he could find a place where they would sell him one), a plastic digital watch and a Yankees cap. He figured they had some of those things in Sundown but Marge seemed to know all the other shopkeepers, and they would tell her about what he had bought (especially the nudie magazine). He also wanted to see a movie, preferably one in which a girl took off her top.

Reg paid for his trip with the money he had won in an essay contest. His entry, called *McLuhan*

Explained, was mainly Media for Dummies. When Marge read it, she frowned and handed it back.

"Where did you learn all those big words?"

He would spend the night at the downtown Bayporte YMCA. He could lift weights there, swim and stay up as late as he wanted. But of course he wouldn't do those things.

Reg sighed as more passengers were getting on the train. At Oxfield, a man boarded and sat next to him.

"It's awfully brisk out there, for this time of year." The man had a few magazines and invited Reg to read one. Reg said that, yes, it did seem cooler than usual. Most of the snow had gone, fortunately.

"Don't you like snow?" the man asked. "I would

rather have snow than rain." He looked around. "At least they keep the train nice and clean. The buses are often filthy. Do you know who owns this railway? The Canadian government. So the people who work here don't exactly make minimum wage."

"I'm not sure how much they like their jobs, though." Reg thought of cranky snack-bar operators and ticket clerks.

"Usually, I drive. I just get into the car and go. Sometimes my parishioners need me immediately, and I try to make myself available to them..."

Reg noticed his dark suit, rather than a collar. The man said he was a Uni-something minister. United Church, Unitarian, Unification...?

"You're not dressed like a minister," Reg said.

"Not today. It's my day off." Then, "I was driving through Evanston, Wyoming one morning and looked up to see both the sun and the moon in the sky. At the same time! It was around dawn, of course, and there was almost no traffic at all, so I was the only one who saw such a sight. I don't imagine it was so unusual, but to me it was the most incredible phenomenon. I actually pulled off to the side and got out of the car to have a nice long look at that sight."

Reg nodded, hoping that no sermon seemed forthcoming about how God was responsible for the sun and moon hanging up there together.

"Quite a thing to see," the man added. "I don't imagine I'll have that pleasure of seeing it again in this lifetime."

The man appeared to be well into middle age. He

was of medium height and strongly built, with clean, ruddy features. He had a full head of silvery hair and smelled of aftershave.

Reg, grateful that the minister would spare him the God-talk, told the minister he'd been a lucky man to see that sight in Wyoming on that special morning.

The man nodded. "Sometimes I think there's so much beauty in the world that I don't want to sleep for fear I'll miss something. Most people don't even bother to look for that beauty, but it's everywhere."

Reg turned towards the window and the minister turned towards his magazines. Reg shivered. The train was chilly. He took his coat off its hook and draped it over himself.

The minister spread his magazines over his lap. Reg thought for a minute that the magazines were touching his leg, then wondered if it was the man's hand. Reg wondered about older, unfamiliar men traveling alone. He thought about Marge, Chicken Hawks and old guys saying they were Good Samaritans. He wondered also about the men who went into Marge's Market, who bought things and delivered things and the men who sat outside on the benches. He thought about the one he would eventually become if he lived long enough.

What if this minister's magazine actually was his hand? Reg moved imperceptibly towards the window, wishing he could metamorphose into Silly Putty and become an inch of goo clinging to the wall of the car. He couldn't tell if the man was touching him, and what could he do about it, anyway?

No. Don't. Please. He screamed silently so that his

head ached but the train rumbled on and nobody heard him. What stopped him from crying out? What was his problem? Embarrassment, humiliation, the uncertainty of what to do next, when the train full of people muttered to each other what was the matter...?

Yes, it was all that, and more.

Reg turned his head very slowly and looked at his neighbor. The man had his head back and eyes closed, his magazines arrayed in his lap. His hand was somewhere in there. Reg swore that hand was touching his young knee, the wrinkled fingers groping firm male flesh, the man's mind delighting in the disgust and terror the boy surely felt.

Take your hand away. Please.

As the train progressed, so did the hand. The man's face stayed so placid that Reg believed the head was asleep but the hand was awake. The boy shuddered, thinking of age and flesh. A Unification minister? Reg pictured the shrewd Korean Reverend Moon with his blank-faced followers, all of them turning over their assets and working to please the Reverend. Reg thought of Roman Catholic priests in the news: stern-faced old men with unholy secrets and desires, bald pates and sagging pallid paunches, awful smells. Worse, shamefully erect phalluses, spread buttocks, old kisses for cute choirboys.

Reg stared out the window and implored the tiny figures of people going about their own lives. Tell him to leave me alone. He thought of the minister's hand, doing as it pleased, daring this boy to defy it. Reg would never permit it. He could stop it whenever he chose to do so. Nothing more would happen.

But he did nothing. As the train entered the tiny

towns close to Bayporte, Reg closed his eyes and breathed slowly, deeply, feeling no power in his own hand to shoo away another's, and no power in his voice to admonish any invasion. Reg could not believe such a violation had happened, was happening or was about to happen. He watched B.C. Flour and Can-Am Foods drift by; he saw the Pacific National Exhibition fairgrounds with its huge rollercoaster and motionless gondola. He had been there once or twice, had spent ten dollars' worth of change throwing darts at balloons on the midway.

He sighed. Soon the train attendant came through, announcing that they would arrive in Bayporte within minutes and they all needed to gather up their possessions. The minister opened his eyes, looked around and arranged his magazines into a tidy stack.

When the train stopped and its doors opened, the

minister hurried out ahead of Reg and disappeared into the crowd. He never saw the man again, to his knowledge, though he thought of him often, whenever he needed someone to despise.

Had he really been a minister, or just another predator—"ready to prey instead of pray," as Marge might have said. Reg always remembered Marge's lessons, regardless of how ludicrous they seemed. She had told him that one of her friends, Carol, worked at the TransCanada Railway Station's souvenir shop.

He entered the lobby, the place of the Chicken Hawks and blue-faced dead women sitting on toilets. He glanced at the Coke machine and shuddered at the thought of wayward boys with knapsacks.

Reg went to the souvenir shop's entrance and debated about to going inside and asking if Carol still worked there. But then he decided he had better things to do, so he left the station and headed over to the YMCA.

Poor Boy

Meredith Dunsmuir fell in love with Reg while both attended Northup University. For him, she was confusing and amazing, incomprehensible. Meredith wanted them to live together. She waited outside his classes, so she was there for him when he finished. If he got into a conversation with his classmates, she would linger, her presence making the others uncomfortable because she was the prettier, smarter and richer than they were. She would listen to what they said, her oval-shaped face inscrutable. When Reg's friend Clark McLellan made an insipid remark about Nietzsche, Meredith arched an eyebrow, nodded in Clark's direction after the boy left and shook her head. "You need to choose your friends more carefully," she said.

Meredith, in her mid-twenties, a graduate student in folklore, stood tall and blonde, with big breasts and an ample bottom. She apologized for being fat (she wasn't, just voluptuous) and said she would make fitness a priority as she got older. Neither her bust nor bottom negated her looks, Reg said to himself. (Something *did* detract from her good looks, at least for him; he had to keep telling himself that he had the prettiest girl around.) She annoyed him with her bouncy walk and swinging arms; Reg thought of her as a flaky beach girl, a bimbo. But she took herself quite seriously. Her family owned Dunsmuir, the upscale department store.

She drove by to pick him up in her yellow Miata, for dates usually consisting of walks through the downtown shopping malls. One time she arrived early and waited in her car, with the top down, windows rolled up and engine running.

"She's out there all alone," said Dr. Meehan, looking out the window. "Poor Meredith." A retired history professor at Northup, he belonged to several committees. Dr. Meehan pitied Meredith because she was young, beautiful, smart and rich, and life would always disappoint her. Peeking out the window, Reg and Dr. Meehan could see her sitting in the car, drumming on the steering wheel.

"Why doesn't she at least come in for a cup of tea?" Dr. Meehan asked. "I think maybe she's dating the wrong fellow."

Reg resented him for saying that. He didn't like how she sat out there in the car, either, not even saying hello to Dr. Meehan. She knew very little about how to conduct herself around others, had no clue that they sniggered behind her back, and Reg felt sorry for her then.

"You're a learned young fellow," Dr. Meehan said one day. "You should read these journals." On the coffee table sat copies of *Canadian Arts and Sciences*, *Partisan Review*, *The New Yorker*, *Maclean's*. Dr. Meehan, once a prominent Northup professor, had written history books that were still required reading at the U. His home, a bachelor's lair full of mahogany paneling and paintings, hardwood floors, made Reg feel cold and uncomfortable most of the time; he wanted to keep his jacket on. To him, Dr. Meehan's fine possessions seemed scarcely better than Marge's *kitschy* stuff in Sundown.

Reg, ambivalent about staying at Dr. Meehan's

home, found the old man a bit too upright and proper, with his meticulous table manners, fine cutlery, modest portions and tiny desserts. Reg always had pocket money for after-dinner walks to the corner delicatessen where, his stomach still he growling, he would devour a sandwich. Dr. Meehan had no pets or cable TV; Reg wanted to spend his evenings playing with a dog or cat, or just space out on music videos. Instead, he had to endure conversations resembling informal quizzes. Had Reg read the great Russian and European authors? An educated young person *needed* to do so. He needed to read the contemporary Americans, too. An erudite man had to know what his political leanings were. Dr. Meehan sneered at capitalism. Reg thought he'd done all right by that system.

Dr. Meehan used words like *indigence* and

lumpenproletariat.

"I guess he meant us," Reg muttered on a visit home.

"What's that?" Marge asked.

"Just talking to myself."

Living with Dr. Meehan made Reg's Sundown visits painful and embarrassing. He had thought little of having Marge's Market in his living room and a repair shop for a garage. Marge's fluorescent lights and acid-trip linoleum floor seemed as good as anyone else's, so what was he to make of Dr. Meehan's mahogany paneling and dark-toned opulence? Reg decided that the two households insulted each other. In Dr. Meehan's rooms, there was always the feeling of museum-like coldness, while in Sundown the rooms fairly reeked of dimestore cheapness, displayed without shame. Poverty, Dr. Meehan believed, wasn't just about having very little money; it was about being vain of trashy possessions. Reg thought of Marge's tall lamp with its Coca-Cola shade she was always dusting.

Anita Feist, his cousin, had given her that lamp and other kitschy things. What would Meredith have thought of such an item, or of Anita Feist?

Anita worked at Cam's Auto Parts. She moaned about the Pakis who had moved into Sundown, especially the Sihk from New Delhi, who worked alongside her and wanted a Cam's of his own one day.

"Maybe you should learn the language before you start worrying about buying Cam's," Anita wanted to tell him. She said that would smarten him up a bit.

Meredith wanted to go to Sundown. "It's close

and we can drive out there. I'd like to see the town and meet your people."

"Well, it's only Marge there now, and most of my friends have moved away," Reg said.

"I wish I could have met your dad, after all the stories you've told me about him."

Reg had told Meredith that his father had been a Renaissance Man and amateur inventor. He didn't tell her about the posthumous Revenue Canada audit and the binders bursting with scribbled nonsense.

"I wish I'd known you back then," Meredith said. "When you were a kid in little old Sundown, surrounded by all those characters."

"You didn't miss anything," Reg said.

"You are a serious young man," Dr. Meehan

sometimes said to Reg, "so you shouldn't be interested in *that*." Usually he meant a Northup football game, a pub crawl, a dance. Reg just shrugged, agreeing that those events did not interest him, but he regretted missing them.

Dr. Meehan kept pictures of the other boys who had stayed in his guest room while attending Northup. Most of them had graduated with honors and become accountants, lawyers and dentists. Reg thought they looked like a bunch of ground-down, nerdy guys with greasy hair and badly knotted ties. He knew that Dr. Meehan wanted to live long enough to say, "You see that picture? His name is Reg, and I helped him become the successful man he is today." Dr. Meehan had helped no actors, TV performers or young hedonists who'd had drunken, naughty good times with wanton women. Reg yearned to become *somebody*, to perform and captivate audiences, to be envied as suave and articulate. He wanted to have fun. He wanted to *be* fun. He wanted to stand on stage and be showered with flowers and cheers and whistles. He wanted people to tell him: You are awesome.

One day he mentioned to Dr. Meehan that he decided he wanted to become a news reporter.

"Well, why not?" replied the retired professor. Meehan. "Unfortunately, Northup doesn't have a journalism program, but you can take all the courses a competent reporter would need. Foreign languages, political science, economics, sociology. The campus newspaper always needs good writers, and I could probably get you an internship somewhere."

Reg considered the Northup campus paper a rag, and all those difficult courses would require more of himself than he wanted to give. He resolved to be less candid around Dr. Meehan. Reg had acquired his housing situation by chance. Another student had occupied Dr. Meehan's guest room until, overcome by stress, he spent a week in Bayporte General Hospital before going back home to Alberta.

Dr. Meehan visited the campus housing office for a replacement. A scholarship student, Reg had gone to the housing office that day, to attend an orientation meeting at Northup's student union building. He learned the facts of university life for the financially challenged: how to earn money, live frugally and maintain good grades.

He got the room number and headed upstairs. The campus, with its considerable sprawl, still confused him; he asked for directions and still got lost. He walked to the office with another scholarship student, swapping a few lies and a couple of truths. Reg did not have a permanent residence yet; he'd gotten a room downtown, at a firetrap called the Gaslight Inn. He had very little money in the bank and expected to struggle for the next four years at Northup, even with his scholarship "You'll definitely need employment," said the other student as they headed towards the orientation session. The other boy, winner of a bursary for computer proficiency. "Get into high tech. That's where the money is. The money, women and power." The high-tech boy, stoop-shouldered and large-nosed, had oily skin and yellowing teeth. He had a soiled knapsack slung over one shoulder and baggy jeans. His grey T-shirt had some sort of faded design on it. He said he wanted to get some sort of part-time job debugging computers. He had a basement suite near the campus. Reg's mind spun with questions about money, women and power.

"This is the place," the boy said, opening an office door.

Inside, Reg immediately thought he'd entered a United Nations meeting. Colored people filled the room: black, white, yellow, brown, red, all with the same expression of working and worrying themselves into early sickness and death. Reg recognized them as the overachievers who'd stayed up all night to make sure they made the highest scores on tests.

Do I, Reg asked himself, look like they do?.

He imagined campus employment: raking the leaves or mopping the floor at the student union building, his brow sweating and muscles burning, while other kids, with far less intelligence but more money, smirked at him as they walked by. Working your way through Northup, eh? Poor baby. Poverty, be it in boys or girls, was unattractive, even pitiful. For girls it could be a bit romantic, if she had beauty and smarts and could be deferential to men, especially the rich young studs who wanted to play Prince Charming to her Cinderella. Was all this relevant to Reg? Did he really give a damn? Yes, it *was* relevant, and he *did* give a damn.

After the meeting, he stood at the top of the stairs and looked down at the swarm of other students, the presumably privileged ones able to do without scholarship checks. They probably did not have to maintain high GPAs, work thankless on-campus jobs or be grateful for the opportunity to one day graduate from Northup. Reg could practically see the kids' pockets bulging with money from Daddy; those boys and girls had no imminent fear of missing out on a

Whistler weekend or pub crawl just because of money. Reg had gotten his school wardrobe, such as it was, from a discount department store, and he envied the people, of whom there seemed to be many, who had gotten their clothes at the Gap or Harry Rosen or Mark James. Before leaving Sundown, Reg had bumped into a neighbor who asked, "Why don't you forget this Northup silliness and just stay here so's you can look after your mum?"

Still at the top of the stairs, he felt someone tap him on the shoulder. He turned around a saw a woman with a kindly face. She said, "Aren't you a scholarship student from Sundown? Don't you need some help with accommodations?"

Reg said yes. She said, "Look, there's someone upstairs you need to meet. Come with me now."

Dr. Meehan was sitting on a vacant desk, chuckling at his own jokes. He liked nothing better than a good conversation, or at least a good audience.

"This could be very good for you," said the woman as she and Reg entered the office. She then dug a fingertip into her own cheek. Reg got the message: Smile, dummy.

By that afternoon, he had moved into Dr. Meehan's spacious guestroom and seen the photos of the young men who had stayed there before him. Dr. Meehan called him a learned young man.

Reg did not have to rake any leaves or clean up after messy students. He did not have to get up at dawn and work till his muscles burned, then study all day. Dr. Meehan got him a job as the advertising coordinator at the *Kodiak,* Northup's campus newspaper. Mainly, he had to deposit advertisers' checks into the college's account and make sure that the ads looked good when they ran in each issue. Many businesses wanted to buy space in the *Kodiak*.

Northup University seemed very old, very big and, on a sunny day, truly majestic. Its buildings were made of brick and stone, its streets were lined with towering elm and oak trees. The school's endowment lands stretched on forever, and the campus itself was surrounded on three sides by beaches and woods. The dormitory rooms were few and cramped, and nearby housing was scandalously expensive. One day, while trimming ads, Reg heard a gentle knock on the door.

"Excuse me, is this the newspaper office?"

"Yes." He stared at the ad in front of him. "This

town has way too many pizza joints."

"Pizza is vile," she said. "I'm here to see about buying an ad."

He looked up and saw a tall, young blonde woman. She said her name was Meredith.

Reg handed her a card. "Those are our rates. The more ads you place, the cheaper it gets."

Meredith made a face. "Ouch!"

"But our circulation is wide and our students have money to spend."

Meredith didn't get her ad, but she did get Reg. Their first meeting happened when he was too distracted to pay her much attention. If he had wanted to capture her interest, he had done an outstanding job. At first, she seemed to have many social-worker instincts Red found incongruous with her beautiful clothes and expensive perfumes. *You poor thing,* she might say if someone complained, or *Aren't some people unkind?* Reg wanted her to think of him as a fiery genius too immersed in the big questions to bother becoming competent at the mundane busywork of everyday life. Instead, he seemed a hapless boy from the sticks, overwhelmed by the task of surviving at Northup.

He saw her regularly on campus and she even occasionally visited the newspaper office. She usually said, "How are you?" as sincerely inquiring into his well-being. She often seemed breathless and blushing when they encountered one another; he thought she struggled with the pressures of graduate school. Later, he discovered it was because she was in love with him.

She found out where he lived, then called him at Dr. Meehan's house and asked him out. "This is Meredith. We met at the newspaper office...?" He said yes. He dated her mostly because Dr. Meehan thought Reg, a learned young man, should be too wise to waste his time with girls and dating.

Soon into their relationship, Reg mentioned to Meredith something about the top news story that day. A college boy, emotionally unstable and in danger of flunking out, had gone to school and shot several students.

"Wouldn't it be weird," he said, "if something like that happened here?"

"That would be tragic. Why would you say such a thing?"

"It happened in the States, so maybe it could

happen here."

Meredith said that down there everyone had access to guns, so they had lots of violent crime.

"Anyway, I'm surprised to hear that sort of talk from you. You're not the sort of boy who would go to school and start shooting people. You just don't have it in you."

"What sort of boy am I?"

"You're a serious young boy who's here on scholarship." Then, "I guess you must think I'm flaky."

Only a very self-assured person could be so outspoken, Reg thought. Meredith flaky? No, he'd been wrong about her.

One time, Reg said, "You and I come from very

different places. Sundown? God, you would hate it. We're poor people."

"I like that. You're charming. You're like the Poor Boy."

"The what?"

"You know, that painting by Hendriksen Gauw. Poor Boy. It's in the Louvre."

Meredith lifted her eyebrows in disappointment. She moved her eyebrows that way when someone failed to know something she knew, or knew something she did not. She believed she knew everything worth knowing. Her brothers, too, seemed annoyed by people who were ignorant of golf, horseback riding and yachting, and they were contemptuous of people who knew about science, technology and business. Meredith and her brothers spoke of trips to Maui and Switzerland as casually as others discussed weekend jaunts to Seattle. The Dunsmuir siblings seemed pompous and modest at the same time. But weren't Anita Feist and Marge, in their own ways, just as bad? Perhaps, but with an essential difference: Meredith and her brothers were insulated and isolated by wealth, while Anita Feist and Marge had to cope with the hassles of everyday life: Pakis in Sundown, Revenue Canada audits, crumbling sidewalks and cracking roads. At the Dunsmuirs' dinner table, Meredith and her siblings whined and moaned about the vegetables served and favorite desserts unavailable. Reg forked food into his mouth, thinking, *You're a bunch of spoiled brats.* They had never needed to shut up, get along or kiss anyone's ass, because they were wonderfully stinking rich and named Dunsmuir.

Reg did not know how much money they had and considered it none of his affair. Fraternity men at Northup, who normally would have laughed at him, shook Reg's hand and congratulated on "winning that Dunsmuir babe," as if Meredith had been a lottery prize worth millions. Naturally, many men had courted her, but only he had possessed whatever she seemed to be seeking. Dr. Meehan, sensing the inevitability of Reg and Meredith's engagement, sat down with him and spoke to Reg.

"It looks as if you are going to marry the heiress to a retail fortune. That's fine; money, as they say, is a nice thing to have." (To which Reg wanted to reply, *You got that right, Professor.*) "But don't lose sight of your own values, goals and beliefs simply because you're marrying into an affluent family."

Heiress to a retail fortune. Meredith at first said

her family had a store, then explained they owned *Dunsmuir*, as if it were Cartier, Tiffany or Rockefeller. Her name meant nothing to him; he had never gone into Dunsmuir, could not have said precisely its location. Grand Street? Roberts Street?

Before visiting Meredith's home, Reg assumed that her family lived in a big house like those in Dr. Meehan's neighborhood. He didn't know about spectacular wealth; to him, rich people were the lawyer or doctor in Sundown, where they would have called him a lucky dog if he had managed to marry or move in with the daughter of the doctor or lawyer.

He found that painting, the Poor Boy. He scrutinized that squatting male, with his big pleading eyes and thick messy hair, the soiled clothes. He supposed he had that sort of swarthy handsomeness. Did Meredith see him that way? Could he be *her* Poor

Boy, and *was* he?

If Meredith wanted to marry him, fine. He would do whatever she wanted, whenever she wanted him to do it. Her money mattered, certainly, but so did the quantity and quality of the love they offered each other. He also believed he would be doing her some sort of favor by marrying her. He saw her love as a tangible object, like a fist-sized lump of gold she had thrust at him; she forced him to take it, or at least hold it with her; she could not bear its weight alone. But Reg had his own wants and needs. And what were they? Love and adoration, mostly, and he believed that Meredith's feelings for him were sincere. He had not gone to Northup looking for love, although he found it there, and he was unlikely ever to encounter a love such as hers again (she knew how lucky he was, too).

Reg, always imaginative and fanciful, had nurtured the belief that someone like Meredith might come along, offering him generous, worshipful love. He also had conceded its unlikelihood. What made a man desirable, it seemed to him, came not so much from who he was as what he had, and how could Reg know what *he* had? In Meredith, he had the woman of his dreams, but not necessarily the woman of his desires. At Dr. Meehan's house, he studied hard and grew cranky. He daydreamed about Meredith's sunny blonde smile, plump breasts and heart-shaped bottom. He reminded himself that he had a beautiful, brainy woman and he needed to be grateful for her. Reg wondered early on why Meredith had chosen to do graduate study at Northup instead of some ritzy foreign college. But then she told him about her undergraduate years at the University of Heidelberg, her honors degree in American studies, her fluency in German. She said nothing more about it, and Reg surmised that her Heidelberg experience had been a disappointment. He knew of few Northup males who had girlfriends, and none of those guys had one he found remotely desirable.

He thought of what she had said: *I must seem very flaky to you.* Then, *Am I the one for you, Reg? Am I the only one?* When he said *Yes, my love,* Meredith, beaming, would compare it to those of the other young couples she knew. Reg shuddered sometimes, after he had spent too many hours with her. They once ended up traipsing through a snowstorm. Meredith, who frequently insisted on holding hands or linking arms with him in public, was strong and determined; she dragged him in her preferred direction. Walking through the snow together that day, Reg dreaded her as someone might cringe at the sight of a favorite meal eaten too often or a funny movie rendered humorless and clichéd by excessive viewings. He wanted to get away from her and shouted, "Race you!" He sprinted towards Meredith's car, which was parked near Dr. Meehan's bedroom window.

She caught up with him. She snaked her arms around Reg's neck and kissed him. She startled him with her tongue, trying to force it into his mouth. When he resisted, she stifled a guffaw. She more than embraced him, she attacked him.

"You're so beautiful," he said to her. "So blonde and magnificent. You're my golden girl."

"No. I'm a rowdy bitch. I'm your slut." She released him, reached down, gathered up some snow and mashed it into his face.

Reg shook it away. She flung some more at him. When he didn't laugh, she started brushing imaginary snow off him. She laughed loudly. He didn't get it.

"Doctor Meehan will hear you," he said.

"Oh, Doctor Meehan, Professor Meehan, Reg is afraid we'll wake you," Meredith called out in a singsong.

"Be quiet."

"Oh, Doctor Meehan, I have something to show you." Meredith quickly unzipped her coat and stuck out her chest at the bedroom window.

"Shut up! You want me to get kicked out?" Reg cried out in a hoarse, desperate whisper.

"You want me to shut up? Make me."

Reg grabbed her from behind, cupping his hand

over her mouth and forcing her to the ground. Then her grabbed a handful of snow and pressed it into her face.

"You like that? Do you? Want some more?"

"Do it some more. It turns me on. I love you, Reg. More than anything."

"No. You're a fucking liar."

Suddenly the bedroom light came on and moments later they heard the window slide open and Dr. Meehan's unforgettable voice.

"Reg, is that you? Is everything all right out there?"

...

"I want to ask you a question," said Dr. Meehan. "Do you love Meredith?"

"Yes," Reg replied.

"And does she return your love?"

"Yes."

Dr. Meehan smiled. "Good. I'm glad. You may actually stand a chance at a happy marriage."

Reg got hungry more often than usual. He wanted junk food: Brownies, corn chips, cookies, Cokes. He got excruciating attacks of acid reflux and gained weight. His best therapy was work. He reread assigned chapters, rewrote term papers. Dr. Meehan was a bit stingy about turning on the furnace, so on many evenings Reg lay awake in bed, chilled and shivering.

...

Meredith moved out of her family's house and rented

a shabby one-bedroom apartment not far from Northup. Reg thought it needed new paint and carpets. She left her underwear and shoes strewn about and waited till her Miata was encrusted with filth before Reg took it to the car wash.

He wondered why she was working so hard on getting a master's degree in folklore. What good would it do her? In the real world, even people with Ph.D.s in the humanities couldn't find teaching positions at community colleges. Her family paid her bills and most of the time didn't bug her. Maybe they knew she would end up working for her family, which was what they wanted.

Reg and Meredith went to her apartment in the early afternoon, when they knew they would be undisturbed for a few hours. They both stripped without ceremony and crawled into her bed. Reg grabbed at her, laughing. Anything to make himself feel less anxious, less terrified of being unable to perform, of seeming vastly inferior to her previous partners. (He had convinced himself that her past was full of handsome European men he wanted never to hear about.) Reg did his best, imagining himself as some sort of porno lover, a good-for-one-thing idiot macho stud, and underneath him Meredith writhed and gyrated, looking through him as he looked past her.

Later, he wanted food. Whatever Meredith kept in her refrigerator was probably inedible. He wanted pasta and Coke. Could they order something in? Did he have enough cash to cover the delivery? (Money, always a difficult matter for him, became more so despite or because of Meredith's willingness to pay whenever he could not.) She wanted to make love some more. She won.

Afterwards, Reg lay alone while Meredith went into the kitchen to make tea. He felt like a pretender, a performer, the way he performed as a drama major at Northup. Could faking it always be so much fun? And was being a pretender altogether such a bad thing? Meredith had been there just for the ride, part of his performance. Reg sometimes believed that any worthwhile woman could fall in love with him. He watched Meredith. He looked around her bedroom, at her Dunsmuir panties and shoes tossed about, her books and other possessions. They seemed ordinary, simple, not a rich girl's things. Maybe, he thought, that could be their goal: to be an ordinary couple, unencumbered by wealth, letting her money remain something distant and isolated, numbers on a bank statement, seldom touched and never taken too seriously. Meredith would have to stop smiling and adoring and touching him so much, although he liked the idea of being so valued by her. She would have to stop her impulsive criticisms and rebukes of him, the huge gaps in his learning, his ignorance of so many things.

But she loved him. What about him did she love? Certainly not his rural accent, which she occasionally mocked. Meredith and her people spoke a crisp, staccato sort of English that was almost British; Reg wanted to tell her, "At least I talk like a Canadian!" His manners were countrified, his outlook limited, his tastes simple. Did she see him as a lump of clay to be modeled into something she wanted?

Reg had so many facets unrelated to accents or manners or clothing. What was she to do about those other parts of him? Still, he wanted her love, wanted it to continue forever. It was the greatest compliment anyone had ever paid him.

They traveled together, to Elizabeth Island, where Meredith's family had a weekend getaway. She had said little to him about them and even less about Reg to them.

He thought she would take him to the family store for some meet-my-folks clothes so he would seem a bit less vulgar to them, but no, she didn't. The Dunsmuirs' home on Great Elizabeth Island had a big, deep-green lawn leading up to a house of stone, timber and stucco. The rear of the house was made of huge windows that looked onto the strait. The floors were hardwood, the ceilings very high. Heft and bulk were all around, even in the water glasses, towels and blankets, as if the owners were afraid the gusty winds would blow everything away. Even the silences were heavy, and soon Reg felt weak, worn out. The meals were substantial and sumptuous, but the effort of eating was almost too much. He had never known that luxury could be such a burden.

They took him on a few walks. Meredith's mother, hugging herself against the icy wind, pointed to the stone wall that separated their property from the next one.

"The stones were imported," she said. "I can't remember where, but it was a long ways off."

"Maybe they should have gotten B.C. stone," Reg said.

To Mrs. Dunsmuir, imported things were always better. What did their store sell? Italian leathers, Swiss timepieces, Irish linens.

"I think they were from Greece or Egypt. The stones," she said.

When he had spent more time around her—as an anthropologist might watch and take notes while feeling baffled by his subject—Reg started to see that she was distant and aloof, dressed in muted colors, as if wanting the world to walk right by her and look right through her. Grandfather Dunsmuir, exploiter of cheap labor, founder of the family business, gazed at his descendants in vivid, oil-based smugness in a portrait hanging in their getaway's living room. Meredith's father, Edgar, was a stocky, gruff, royally arrayed man. His sons had drifted in and out of colleges, had tried this and that career, spent countless thousands of dollars on extended vacations abroad. He yelled mostly at them, then started in on Meredith.

"How are your folklore studies going?" he asked

at the dinner table. "If you're so bloody smart, why don't you make yourself useful at the store?"

"Business is boring," she said.

"Folklore is useless," he said.

"Folklore is culture." Meredith practically snarled at him. "There's more to life than selling overpriced clothes to insecure people. You couldn't begin to understand."

Todd and Russ, Meredith's brothers, asked Reg about his hobbies. Did he golf, ride horses, play tennis, travel...? "What do you do?"

"This and that," Reg said.

"Where do you go?"

"Here and there. But mostly I just hack around."

"Maybe he's a scholarly genius like Meredith," said Todd.

"Maybe he studies folklore," their father interjected.

Meredith later told Reg that her father got cranky when business was bad, and when it was good, he seemed angry that it wasn't even better. He got mad at his sons because they spent far too much time and money on their fun and games instead of getting off their lazy asses and making something of themselves. Back in Sundown, Reg's people were hardly without flaws, but their complaints seemed more in the nature of being teasing towards each other, while Edgar Dunsmuir, full of privilege, was also truly malicious.

Reg and Meredith lay on the beach and embraced. They tried to do more but gave up and whispered to each other.

"Your family doesn't like me," he said.

"They don't like *us*. What we have." She paused. "Now do you understand?" Meredith asked him. "Now do you understand why I need you?"

Later on, they went to Sundown. Reg thought it was an extraordinarily bad idea but Meredith insisted that they go. It was a disaster. Marge cooked them up a huge dinner of perogies, onions, sausage and liver. The portions were huge and Meredith's face turned blue as she stared down at the steaming mound of country food placed before her. Some of the good was a gift from Anita Feist, who joined them for this feast.

She knew, and by now so did everyone else, that Reg was engaged to Meredith Dunsmuir. He also knew that Anita would go to work the next day filled with stories about her "dinner with the millionaire chick" and how she, Anita, impressed the hell out of Cousin Reg's fancy fiancée.

"Well, we just welcomed her with open arms, filled her tummy with the best food she'd ever tasted and then we told her what's what in Sundown."

Reg knew that Marge would have fun telling her customers about Meredith's inability to "clean her plate" and other failings. He knew Marge would have great fun imitating Meredith's bulging eyes and "Oh God I can't eat all this" facial expression. But at the dinner table Reg and Meredith simply did their best to get through the meal. Reg tried to begin a conversation about the changes in Sundown, sounding enthusiastic, asking questions of Marge and Anita Feist, who mainly just shrugged and kept staring at Meredith. He felt...what? Ashamed. Of the coarse country food on his plate and the cheap trinkets ubiquitous in Marge's kitchen. He was ashamed for Meredith, who just sat wiping her nose and picking at her food. But mostly he felt ashamed of himself, for feeling unable to be himself despite sitting in the house in which he had grown up. Sitting alongside Meredith, he couldn't speak his natural way without sounding like a hick to her; at Northup, especially when spending time with her, he was always trying to sound like those around him: urban, educated. But now, at the dinner table with Marge and Anita Feist, he cringed at the sound of their cornpone twangs. To the Sundowners, talking was yelling, interrupting, browbeating, using words and syllables to smack each other across the face. They expected you to nod that you understood them, even if you disagreed. *I seens you on the street the other day.* They actually said such things. Reg, sitting there next to Meredith and imagining what he must be hearing and seeing, could only roll his eyes and wait it all out.

He asked Marge about the changes she had seen in Sundown, thinking that Meredith might be interested in hearing about such things. Marge began to talk, seeing that the floor was hers, and she spoke of some things that interested her.

"The bridge that takes you to Brandiz? They've had people jumpin offin it almost as much as they jumped off into the Golden Gate river in the States."

Marge was particularly interested in suicides at that time. She went on about how over a thousand people had leapt off the Golden Gate Bridge in San Francisco. Marge knew how fast they traveled (about

70 miles per jour), how many seconds it took them to hit the water (seven) and the likelihood of surviving the fall (80 percent didn't make it). Coast Guard boats were usually the ones who fished the corpses out of the water, and some of the bodies were quite a grisly sight to behold.

"This *was* a bad idea," Meredith conceded on the drive back to Bayporte. "What a creepy place. I'm sure you're glad you don't live there anymore."

Reg resented her for saying that.

"I know that woman isn't your mother," she said. "She must make you miss your mother terribly, even if you didn't actually know her." She sighed. "My poor Reg."

Reg resented that, too, even though he agreed with her. *You're such a phony,* he wanted to say to Meredith, although he knew he was even phonier, with his inability to sit proudly with his own people and introduce them to the woman he was going to marry. In the future he would learn to use Sundown to his advantage, making fun of it to amuse some people and bragging about it to impress others. But that would come later; for now, he felt shame and queasiness.

His Sundown pride was beginning to happen. Now that he had Meredith's promise of a new and bountiful life, he clung to memories of Marge's Market, the Jessop Valley and myriad other things while Meredith took him smugly through her world of tony stores, big houses and the ocean she seemed to think she owned.

...

They went to Monticello Jewelers downtown and Meredith picked out a diamond ring. Reg sat and watched as his fiancée took out her American Express card.

She's paying for her own ring and I don't even know how much it costs._What's wrong with this picture? he thought.

That evening, she told him that as soon as she graduated from Northup she would go to work full time at Dunsmuir. Her father was going to buy them a house.

"What will you do at the store?" Reg asked.

"I don't know. But I'm sure they can make room for one more. I need to work now that I have a husband to support."

"Will we have a house like the one your parents

live in?" he asked.

"No."

He smiled. "Good."

"We'll find a place we both like." She let out a long sigh. "I'm so sick of school. You can stay there and graduate. Become a professional student."

Reg chuckled. "Won't your parents disapprove?"

"They won't care. I don't really think they see you as part of our family. You're just sort of my live-in boyfriend. I have this ring and we'll have this piece of paper, but it doesn't mean anything to them."

"Oh."

. . .

When he went back to Sundown, to see Marge, he

learned that she had told everyone about his engagement to Meredith. The barber said, "You're Marge's boy, eh? You're goin to marry the Dunsmuir girl? Always glad to see a local boy go into the big city and make good."

When people said he must be thrilled, he said he was, and some of those people said successful, as if he'd climbed Mount Meredith. He said he was happy, thrilled. He beamed and nodded and shrugged and played his part with ease. Will you live in West Shore, they asked, and is it really as nice as everyone says?

"Yes, yes!" Reg cried. "It's awesome!"

When Reg awoke and couldn't get back to sleep, he saw that the sky was getting the tiniest bit lighter. So he got dressed, let himself out of Dr. Meehan's house and started the long walk to Meredith's apartment, unsure if the buses were still running. It didn't matter. He felt like walking. Bayporte, for a big city, went to bed early and nothing really opened until nine-thirty. Dr. Meehan lived in a fashionable neighborhood, not absolutely stinking rich like West Shore, but filled with coffee shops and other hangouts for upwardly mobile young people seeking rich spouses. Reg had gotten a rich girl who wanted to marry him, without seeking one.

As she opened her door, Meredith scratched her backside and stifled a yawn. "Reg? Why are you here? Do you know what time it is?"

"Meredith," Reg said, stepping inside and taking her into his arms. "Let's not get married."

"What?"

"I don't want to get married."

"Well." Meredith ran a hand through her long shiny hair and took a deep breath. Morning was her worst time; she woke up with dark circles under her eyes and a muzziness that wouldn't lift until she'd showered and had breakfast. He'd come over to explain something that would make no sense to her, and there would be no good time or place for this conversation.

"Let's sit," she said.

"No. I feel like a jackass right now. I don't want to get married."

"This is the first time you've said anything about it."

"I've been thinking about it a lot."

"Do you have HIV or something? Are you

dying?"

"Don't be funny." Reg closed his eyes and took a deep breath.

"Well, then...?"

"I don't love you. Never have, never will." He sat on her bed. "I can't go through with this."

Meredith waited a few minutes and said. "There's no reason for us

to get married if you don't want to. There's no law against it. But I'm just wondering if you *really* know right now what you want. Couples do that all the time. They ask themselves if this huge commitment they're making is the right thing."

"I know this," he said slowly. "I don't want to marry you. Our whole relationship has been wrong for both of us."

"If you say so, Reg."

Meredith's beautiful blonde face looked hard and cold. Reg, feeling empowered, said more.

"Why should we get married? What reason do we have? We have nothing in common. You think I'm white trash and you're somehow doing the world a favor by marrying me. Well, no thanks, I don't need your pity."

"I fell in love with you, Reg. I wanted to marry you."

"You're just a snob," he said. "You're just a phony." He stood up and thought of more to say.

"You're not even that good a lover. I didn't want to get involved with you in the first place. It was all your idea. I pity you. It's like you're

always in your own little dream world, you've had every possible advantage and you've got nothing on your mind except Number One. You brag all the time and look down your nose at everyone else, but you don't seem to understand that everyone else is laughing at you."

They stared at each other for several long seconds. Meredith nodded the tiniest bit, as if giving him permission to continue. He had more things to say but thought better of it. He stalked out of her apartment but closed the door quietly so as not to wake her neighbors.

Meredith sent him an email: "I'm not sure what happened to us the other morning but let's talk about it after we've had a week or so to get our thoughts together."

Reg wondered if Meredith could get her money back from the jeweler. He didn't say anything to Dr. Meehan about Meredith and didn't want to see the smug look on the old man's face about the broken engagement. He just studied and tried to forget about everything else for the time being.

He went to Northup and pretended as if nothing had changed. He avoided those people who might ask about Meredith. His relationship with her had made him a Big Man on Campus. Unused to being envied, Reg wanted to keep his special status for as long as he could.

He thought, What now?

Leaving Dr. Meehan's home seemed the sensible thing to do. If he was serious about cutting Meredith loose, he could somehow find the courage to move out of Dr. Meehan's home. Should he withdraw from Northup, too? He cringed at the idea of being on campus and hearing, "Too bad you blew your thing with Meredith, eh?"

Reg would have to find employment. Downtown, in the Financial District, they always wanted administrative assistants and office flunkies. He could apply at the hotels, restaurants and gift stores. If they hired him, would they fire him two weeks later?

Everyone has one special thing they can do, he'd heard someone say in a movie. Reg's one special thing was school work. He told himself: Forget about go-nowhere jobs downtown. Stay at Northup. On one weekend day at the campus library, he was on the staircase, halfway up, where he had a perfect view of everyone on the floor below him. He saw Meredith in one of the cubicles and was pretty sure she couldn't see him. He gazed at her tumble of blonde hair, yellow crewneck pullover, faded jeans. He no longer felt threatened by or resentful of her; he could admire her as he would any other pretty girl on campus. She had been a good sport about their breakup, had thrown no tantrums. She had neither stalked him nor tried to make trouble. Having accepted his rejection, she would soon find another man, perhaps a rich and classy guy who would not embarrass her the way Reg had. He felt disgusted with himself now over the things he had said to her, especially his remarks about her lovemaking. Who was he to criticize her, anyway? Reg was so pleased at seeing her again that he wanted to give her some sort of parting gift, a gesture of admiration and goodwill that she could remember and smile about long afterwards.

Standing on the stairs, he pictured himself running down to Meredith, throwing his arms around her, his tears soaking her sweater as he planted a thousand sweet kisses on her neck, saying, *I love you! I always have and always will! Can you ever forgive me? Say you'll love me forever!* The temptation for him to do such a thing burned like acid in his veins. He felt a mad desire to bound off the staircase and rush over to her, and give them a second chance.

While trying to talk himself out of it, he went ahead and did it. Much later, when Reg read self-help books that instructed him to reach out to others, he told people about this time in his life. He spoke to everyone who would listen, from party acquaintances to single-serving friends sitting next to him on flights. He talked so openly to acquaintances because he assumed he would almost certainly never see again.

Often, they told him things about themselves, too. When they asked him why he "resurrected" his relationship with Meredith, he said it was out of "avarice," and that she had "resources." He was young, naïve and unskilled; what were his options as a single man? When socializing with practical-minded people, Reg would say that only rich people had choices in life; everyone else had to live with the choices the wealthy had given them. If he'd had the price of a ticket back to Sundown, his life would have turned out differently.

Later, he would change his mind about his reasons for getting back together with Meredith. It was a matter of power, he would say. Why get her back? Because I could. But their life together had been difficult. They were married for about a dozen years, fighting often and passionately, taking the same cruel, verbal cheap shots at each other.

Reg fears that he has told people about using a golf club to smash a window in his house, slamming his fists into walls, then cowering on the sofa, blubbering for his wife's forgiveness (which she always provided). He dragged her by her hair; she bruised him all over with punches and kicks. The next morning, they would make a special breakfast of seafood omelets and gourmet coffee and giggle about the shattered dinnerware and upended furniture.

Why did you fight like that? people asked.

Maybe we didn't love each other enough. Or we loved each other too much. Their shrinks suggested time together and apart. Role playing, fair fighting. Some of it worked, in the beginning. Most of the couples they knew who fought claimed fighting was therapeutic Reg and Meredith could not part until they had hurt each other past the point of forgiveness.

He told no one of the other thing that kept him together: a simple vision or expectation of bliss. After telling people these horror stories, he could not add that there were times of stability and happiness in his marriage: times of having a child, going shopping, enjoying simple things. He sought out those times and wished to prolong them, as if he saw another Reg and Meredith, their *doppelgangers*, just a few feet away, a content couple they could aspire to emulate. Maybe it was that Meredith, the happy phantom, he had seen that day in the campus library as he stood on the stairs. He should have just left her there in that cubicle.

He met up with her again, years later, long after

their divorce. Reg saw Meredith in the Los Angeles International Airport bar. By then he had become a moderately famous journeyman actor who flew to southern California for TV and film work. He entered the bar just after midnight, on his way back to Bayporte, alone, exhausted, resigned to a sleepless flight and a solitary taxi ride home. To Reg, the LAX bar, always open, was a refuge from the little black boys in Dodgers gear who relentlessly panhandled him. The City of Angels and its little devils intimidated him. He sat nursing a highball at a corner table when he spotted Meredith entering the bar. She had replaced her hippie earthiness with slick corporate polish. She wore a dark blue suit and her hair was shorter and blonder than remembered. But she was still unmistakably Meredith, whom he regarded as a familiar face, someone he would always know. He felt embarrassed about his own slovenliness, his graying hair, darkening shadow and rumpled raincoat. He stared at her until she looked in his direction.

He smiled.

She scowled. She made a face filled with the most abject contempt, loathing and disgust. Hard to believe, but unmistakably there. Reg swallowed and shifted in his seat. Occasionally when playing a scene in front of movie cameras, Reg would get the feeling that the other actor wanted to make a face, scowling or sneering or smirking, and the actor could be an aging Oscar winner or an overeager upstart, and the face they wanted to make was usually meant to enhance their performance as well as to call attention to themselves. But they didn't make that face because the director would yell "Cut!" and order another take, and the take with the face in it would never be printed.

Reg drained his drink in a swallow and hustled out of the bar and down the endless airport corridor, breathless. She had *scowled* at him.

Who, really, could do such a thing?

Meredith could. She could do everything.

GEORGE ONSTOT

BAD REGGIE

Reg fell in love with Twyla, the hostess of the party he and Meredith attended. Her husband was Willem, and they had been married about five years, a couple of years longer than Reg and Meredith. Willem and Twyla lived across the river and up in the hills. They had a magnificent view of practically everything worth seeing, although their house itself was smaller and shabbier than the ones surrounding it. The party was in June; Meredith drove through rain and wind across the bridge. Reg wanted to turn back—this party was too far away, he didn't the people who would be there, and everyone would just sit or stand around, bitching about the June rainstorm. He wanted to turn on the radio but Meredith, squinting and muttering through the rain-spattered windshield, would just turn it off. She had dressed him in a baggy leather jacket and pleated khaki slacks, because she didn't trust him to dress himself and she wanted the other guests to think he was both rich and funky. She wore a short, low-cut black evening gown. Reg thought they looked as if they were going to a Halloween party, dressed as a socialite who'd picked up a hitchhiker. He did not know that this evening would change his life. Meredith felt anxious about these outings, too, although she was usually reluctant to say so. Their ambivalence happened for different reasons. Meredith was a Dunsmuir and Reg a nobody. Her friends were actually her family's friends, and felt she and Reg should have their own friends. It seemed to him that they collected friends, the way other people collected porcelain ducks or wicker furniture. He sometimes saw Meredith as part of some collection, a store-bought princess, heiress to a retail fortune, on his arm and with him in bed for reasons that mystified him. They accepted invitations often, and had people over when they felt they should.

This evening at Twyla and Willem's, the guests were artsy-fartsy Northup types, garrulous people Reg and Meredith had never met. He was told that one man at the party had directed a hugely unsuccessful feature film. He expected them to be smart, demanding, ambitious people who, even at a party, competed to see who could say the funniest things or make the most profound observations.

Reg wondered how these people, especially the

men, would react if he told them that he had married
the pretty blonde in the evening dress, who happened
to be the Dunsmuir heiress. Would they have cared?

The first time Reg saw Twyla was when she was
in the maternity ward, reading a copy of Saul Bellow's
Herzog. At that time she was reading all the top
American contemporary authors. Reg meant to read
Bellow's work and thought he might ask to borrow
Twyla's copy.

Probably the things he liked most about Twyla
were her ponytail, glasses and hoodie, as she were one
of the Northup coeds who filled the campus library
every afternoon. She certainly didn't act like a first-
time mother, silent and frowning as she read. The
woman in the bed next to her kept thinking aloud

about Dr. Spock's books on infant care.

Meredith was drowsy most of the time and Reg thought she and Twyla were having a good-natured competition over who could cope better in the ward.

Meredith told Reg that she dreamed of being confronted by an infant screaming and crying.

"Give the kid its bottle and change it and it'll be fine," he said.

While his wife slept, Reg got acquainted with Twyla. Her husband was a musician and she was a dancer.

"Twyla, are you reading Doctor Spock three times a day?" Reg asked.

"At least," she said. "Sometimes I manage four or five."

"Keep it up," he said. "That good old man will make a decent mother of you."

She laughed. "I doubt it."

"And do you make sure you wear your sterilized gloves while you read Dr. Spock?"

"Yes. I know how bacteria thrive on paper."

So they became friends, the way people do in prison, school or church. They sat in the hallways reading magazines even after nurses asked Twyla to go back to bed. During these hours Reg and Twyla did not read Saul Bellow or James Joyce but the trashy movie magazines they found lying on the tables.

"It says here that most people in the movies have had plastic surgery."

"Most people? I'd say everyone in the movie business has had some work done."

"They also have fake hair."

"Fake tits."

"Fake balls."

The Dr. Spock woman said they were being rude and disgusting, with their loud laughter and cynicism. She said that if they didn't pipe down and mind their manners, they might be asked to leave the hospital. She said she couldn't be sure about it, but it seemed to her that women who talked loud and were impolite didn't turn out to be the best mothers.

Twyla said she would put her kid up for adoption if the little bugger got to be too much trouble to have around.

"You're awful," said the woman.

After that, Reg and Twyla began their sentences with *I can't be sure about it, but...*

"I can't be sure about it, but this food doesn't appear to be edible," she said.

"I can't be sure about it, but I think that being a parent will be rather time-consuming," Reg said.

Twyla told Reg that she was twenty-three and this would be her only child. Her daughter, in fact, had been an accident; she and Willem simply had no desire for children, but now they had one. Willem, she said, was a workaholic musician.

"He is gifted. He can pick up virtually any instrument and learn to play it in under an hour. That's why he doesn't visit me very often. He's so busy with his work. I'm glad he doesn't come by that often. He would just piss me off."

She said little about money but Reg guessed that Willem's people were well off. Twyla was from the Midwest. Her father was a warehouseman and her mother taught piano. Reg said he came from a small town several hours away and had met Meredith at Northup.

"'Sundown'?" Twyla asked. "I've never heard of it."

"Neither has anyone else."

"What does Meredith do?"

"She's smart for a living," he said.

Twyla smiled. "Nice for her. Why didn't you have your kid in a place better than this?"

"Because we've just bought a house and want to economize a little bit."

"Sounds great. New kid, new house. Aren't you thrilled?"

"Overwhelmed."

Twyla told him about life with her neurotic mother.

"She discouraged me from having any masculine tendencies. Everything was very frilly in my bedroom and she forced me to collect dolls. Then she got me into dance classes. I was tall and muscular, so it came to me easily enough and I've sort of made a career out of it. Willem is a musician, one of the best around. He is musically gifted and can play most instruments. We're both slobs."

"Mozart was a slob, too."

"Men can get away with things."

"Yes."

Twyla espoused the ideas of the progressive young women of her era, and found Reg refreshingly lacking in sophistication. He got a bit offended and reminded her that he had a theatre degree from Northup University. Twyla's face became colored by a deep blush and an embarrassed grin. She said, gently, that a Northup education was no education at all. Reg spent time with Willem, too. The man seemed to live inside his own head, composing music to himself while trying to conduct the business of everyday life. Reg decided that Twyla and Willem were a mismatch, and figured that they felt the same way about his marriage to Meredith.

At the party, Reg felt relieved that Meredith wasn't overdressed. She had sweated off all her post-baby flab and looked ravishing. Despite the heavy rain the humidity was high and people were dressed lightly. Reg felt good, being at a party with Meredith and seeing her comfortable amid unfamiliar people. Occasionally they could have a good outing together, but other times were less enjoyable.

While studying at the U., she had taken him to the Museum of Contemporary Art and shown some appreciation for whatever was on display. She did so because the Dunsmuir family was publicly supportive, but privately contemptuous, of artists, and she wanted to alienate her family.

On one afternoon at the museum, they spent an

hour in a huge room filled with Robert Mapplethorpe nudes. Reg stared at the floor, wondering why she wanted him to look at pictures of naked men. Meredith had been cranky all week and made sneering judgments about Mapplethorpe's context and symmetry. *Well, at least she's picking on this fag photographer and not me*, Reg thought. He had a very open mind and was willing to listen to others. Meredith didn't have that problem.

After a handful of emotionally vicious marital fights, Reg did his best to placate Meredith. She often berated him over some innocent question or casual comment. In the hope of flattering her with deference, he would seek her opinion on some subject that interested her. He wanted to listen to her and admire her erudition and eloquence, but she might speak to him in a voice sharp with impatience.

God! How stupid are you?

Reg wanted to admire and respect his wife, and sought opportunities to do exactly that. He believed he did respect, admire and love Meredith, though not in the way he felt a husband should. He had convinced himself that she had no desire to make the journey her family had put her on. They had given her everything she wanted, everything she had asked for, and none of it seemed to make her happy. Poor little rich girl. A few of the men at Twyla and Willem's party wore mock turtlenecks and faded jeans like the Silicon Valley CEOs who had become twenty-something zillionaires. The higher up you went, the more you dressed down. Twyla and Willem had stuffed their refrigerator with American beer. Reg thought of a joke: "No, Officer, I'm fine. I've been drinking Budweiser all night." After several beers, Reg went to piss, then headed into the kitchen for more to drink.

Someone introduced him to the man who had directed the disastrous film.

"I liked your movie." Reg said.

"No, you didn't. It sucked." Yes. Reg and Meredith had left the cinema revolted and confused. The film seemed to be about an eccentric, graying musician who spoke to sharks and whales through his compositions. Reg dismissed it as bullshit and forgot about it. Meredith admired the performance of the music composer, but the female lead, playing a greedy ex-wife, seemed to have walked in from another movie altogether.

"Awful." The director shook his head. "I nearly sued to get my name off the film." He added that the star was always drunk and the actress playing the ex-wife was in a snit over her real-life lover. "The publicity budget was zilch and nobody knew the movie even existed," he said.

"Hard luck." Reg looked at the empty beer bottle he was holding and wondered if it would be rude just to open the refrigerator and get another one.

"Dead soldier?" Twyla asked, taking the empty bottle and getting him a full one. "Yummy," she said, looking at Reg and licking her lips.

Yummy?

Maybe she was just flirting. That was OK; he liked getting that sort of attention from other women. Maybe she flirted with the women, too. Reg thought for a moment that this might be a kind of Halloween party after all; everyone was being someone else. Reg was not an affable oaf from Sundown right now. He was one of the hip, prosperous people who snubbed Sundowners.

Some man and his date were making out in a corner. He kept one hand squeezing her breast and seemed to be trying to suck her tongue out. Reg cringed. He loathed public displays of affection; he didn't even like holding Meredith's hand in front of other people.

A skinny little guy named Basil stood by the bathroom, chatting up the women who were waiting to go in. "This is a good way for us to get to know each other," he said.

"Basil is obnoxious," said the movie director. "Years ago he published a poem in The Southern Gothic Review, and ever since then he tries to be tragic and overbearing like Poe."

"He's succeeding," said Reg. They all laughed, and he felt pleased with himself for saying it.

They heard raised voices coming from the living room. A man presently stepped into the kitchen, looked at Reg and pointed to the living room.

"Your old lady is really pissing them off in there."

Meredith was going on about Quebec and national unity. "So Quebec wants to become a separate country? Well, fuck them. Let the bastards go. We're better off without them. In fact, we should *insist* that they secede."

If you think she's running her mouth now, Reg thought, you should hear talk about AIDS, drug addiction, capital punishment and gays in the military.

"Well, they *are* a separate and distinct society. Their culture is a precious thing. We should be proud of them," said a nervous young man whose discomfort with Meredith's brashness merely provoked her further.

"Bull*shit*." The room became hushed. "They are not a 'separate and distinct society.' They are just a bunch of assholes. They work in Canada. They screw and have babies in Canada. Then they spit in our faces and threaten to become a foreign country."

"Have you ever even been to Quebec or known any people there?" asked the nervous young man.

Meredith had been to Quebec many times. Her family was opening a store in Montreal.

"Well," she said, "those people need to be slapped around and told to stop whining. They need to grow up."

"Really?" asked another partygoer.

"Fucking right." Meredith nodded. "They need to stop watching French-language TV and learn English. French is bullshit."

Reg closed his eyes and disappeared onto the porch. He looked out into the foggy, drizzly night. Bayporte would be the perfect place, he told himself, if it didn't rain so goddamn much. Meredith's performance degraded and angered him. What arrogance! Didn't she know that she was just making a fool of herself? Him, too.

Still, he didn't understand why people got so riled up about Quebec. Let the Quebeckers secede from Canada, negotiate a separation agreement with Ottawa. Hearing the talk and laughter inside the house, he wondered if he should go back in and show them that Meredith and he had no separation agreement.

She had some ugly opinions, but he believed she had a beautiful soul. Reg reminded himself: My wife has a beautiful soul. My wife *is* a beautiful soul. He heard footsteps and continued staring out at the dark gray sky. Twyla came out. She didn't say anything; neither did he. Twyla. He stood looking out at the nighttime sky as she wrapped her arms around his waist and rested her chin on his shoulder.

"I'm lonely," she murmured. "Are you lonely, too?"

"A little bit." For several minutes they stood there, kissing and groping. When they went back inside, Basil said, "I was going to send out a search party if you didn't come back in another two minutes."

"We had an affair," Twyla said.

"Glad I came?" Reg asked her.

She smirked. "You didn't. But we can work on that."

They said very little to each other for the rest of the evening and stayed on opposite sides of the room, but every few seconds they scanned the room, making eye contact. Reg's heart sped up. Twyla seemed an abundant and womanly presence, generous and welcoming. She usually had a tan from a downtown glass bed; she went skiing as often as she could to stay lean. Twyla had told him about her lifelong weight concerns, her bullying classmates, her morbid fear of age and death.

The morning after the party, Reg, Meredith and June sat eating breakfast when the phone rang. Reg answered it.

"I hope you didn't stay up all night thinking about me," said Twyla.

"We had a nice time," Reg said. "Thanks for having us over."

"Our private visit? That was for real."

"I know." Reg's wife and their daughter were forking food into their mouths, oblivious to the phone call. Their kitchen was a spacious vision of whites and creams, too big for this small family. It was Meredith's; ultimately, Reg was a houseguest. He could lose his privileges, be out on his ass, if he did the wrong things.

"It's beautiful outside today," he said. "We were trying to think of something fun to do."

"Is Meredith in the room?"

"Yes."

"Ouch. Bad time to call you, eh? I'm at work, in my leotard. I just wanted to hear the sound of your voice."

"OK."

"We'll get together soon." She made a kissing sound. Click.

"Was that Willem or Twyla?" Meredith asked.

"Twyla. She just wanted to make sure we didn't get mugged on the way home."

"Twyla." Meredith sighed.

"Twyla's nice." Reg liked speaking her name in his home, filling the kitchen air with the sound, praising the absent woman in front of his present wife. Twyla, Twyla, Twyla.

"Why did she have to call on Saturday morning?"

"She's an artist. They keep weird hours," Reg said.

"She's weird. Too competitive," said Meredith. "She competes like a man. She looks like one, too. Don't you think so?"

"I don't know. I'll have to pay more attention to her."

. . .

Twyla called again a few days later. "We finally got all picked up after that party. You know what slobs we are. What a hassle. But the party was fun."

"My missus got a little carried away," said Reg.

Twyla chuckled. "Oh, *that?* She provided a floor show. Free entertainment."

"You get what you pay for." Reg felt surprised at how easily, and critically, he and Twyla spoke of Meredith. He no longer saw any need to defend her against others; he enjoyed hearing her critics.

Willem played for the philharmonic and got session work. His family owned the house with the great view, and Reg guessed Willem's people sent him and Twyla a monthly check. Meredith said little about her sales job at the family store, and she seemed sick of it already. But so what? She had the easiest job in town; Dunsmuir's suits, shoes, wallets and hats sold themselves, especially when the voluptuous blonde looking after you happened to be a Dunsmuir.

The more time he spent with Twyla, the more he felt that he and Willem should swap wives. Willem and Meredith had come from moneyed families who considered wealth the greatest of all possible blessings. Reg and Twyla were charming nobodies who had gotten lucky.

What would Meredith do if she fell in love with another man? First, probably go to see her lawyer about the financial cost of making Reg go away. She didn't believe in shrinks and pills and pity parties. If loving Meredith meant seeing something vital and worthwhile and wonderful inside her, his love for Twyla (if indeed it was love) was a very different experience. Reg believed his love for Meredith came from his faith in her innate superiority to him; she was above committing adultery. With Twyla, he could be shameless and faithless without any feeling any obligation. What, exactly, did Reg want with Twyla? Not much: just surprises, variety, an erotic adventure. He wanted more gropes, like the one he'd had with her on her back porch in the drizzle.

...

Later that year, Reg lay awake in the middle of the night. Meredith, splayed out beside him, was a heavy, grateful sleeper in their huge, airy bedroom. He had made plans to spend the following night with Twyla, whose ballet troupe was rehearsing in Mason River, about an hour away. Reg, staring at the bedroom ceiling, was ambivalent about actually meeting up with Twyla for carnal pleasure. Cheating was too different from what he was used to, too inconvenient, too incongruous with his "Sundown values." Reg and Twyla had kept in close touch since the party but had not yet consummated their relationship.

Something had made them hold back; both had spouses, responsibilities. Her car wouldn't start, her period had.

Twyla's work took place in different locations and irregular hours; Willem would believe whatever she said about where she'd been and what she had been doing. She finally offered Reg a plan: a rendezvous in separate cars, dinner downtown and a romp in one of the local hotels.

Reg and Twyla once sat kissing in a downtown café, with his arm looped around her neck, until the server came by and told them to cool it. Another time, Twyla met up with Reg and June at a local park. The two adults sat at a bench holding hands while the little girl frolicked. June surprised them by saying,

"Hah! Naughty, naughty!"

"What do you mean by that? 'Naughty, naughty'?" Reg asked.

She made a kissing sound. "You were doing what mommies and daddies do."

"Wanna go get a milkshake? Chocolate? Strawberry? We'll get extra-large."

He knew bribing his child to keep her mouth shut would happen again, many times. June would probably end up on a counselor's couch, wondering why daddies did naughty things and bribed their daughters to shut up about them. Reg dozed for an hour before waking up. He pulled himself out of bed, looked out the window and smiled at the clear sky. He'd lied to Meredith that one of his old friends from the U. was going to Seattle for a conference and Reg was driving down there for a reunion; if it gottoo late, he would just stay at the hotel hosting the conference. His explanation sounded insipid to him even as he spoke it, but Meredith just nodded, distracted.

Reg checked his wallet and counted his money. If the Dunsmuir family was rich, Reg was not. They had given him an American Express card, identical to Meredith's, to use for discretionary spending. If he got a cash advance on the card, he would get a call from their accountant. The card and the accountant irritated him in much the way that he and Meredith irritated each other. Since falling for Twyla, Reg had languished in an inert compatibility with Meredith that, to other people, probably resembled marital bliss. Reg decided he would have to use cash for this tryst. He couldn't risk using his in-laws' AmEx card at some no-tell motel. He wandered into the living room, an *Architectural Digest* scene of grey, green and silver. One whole wall was made of stone; the sofas were made of a weird fuzzy material. He liked the Royal Doulton clown figurines on the mantel. Four clowns, each with a crazy garish smile. They're laughing at me, he thought. Well, I deserve it. Keep laughing, boys. Each day, he checked to make sure that nobody had moved them.

"Who's been dicking around with these clowns?"

"Just me," Meredith replied. "As soon as you leave the house, I toss them around. Sometimes they break, so I Goofy Glue them back together and hope you won't notice."

"Meredith, be serious. Does June touch them? You know how kids are. They think everything's a toy."

Bored and rich, Meredith and her mother bought things and tried them out in this house. Whenever people came by—and, to Reg, they seemed mainly to ogle Meredith and snicker at him—Meredith would take them through the house with a realtor's exuberance. Gee whiz!

Reg sat in the living room while Meredith showed off the house: its vast entryway, recessed lighting, skylights, hardwood floors. Then she took them into their modest backyard and waved her arms at an imaginary swimming pool.

"Imagine! All that money for this house and no pool! Can you believe it?"

Reg wondered why he hadn't heard from Twyla. Finally she called. She sounded matter-of-fact.

"When will you arrive in Mason River?" he asked.

"I don't know. This afternoon sometime. You should drive down there now because there may be a long lineup at the border."

"Where will we stay?" Reg asked.

"We'll find someplace. Those border towns are packed with hotels."

She had told the others in the troupe that she would be spending the night with some friends in Mason River.

"I want to see you dance," Reg said.

"Okay."

"Are you sure?"

"Reg..."

"You sound ambivalent."

"No. I'm here with the other dancers now..."

"And they all think I'm Willem."

"Yes," she said.

Reg arrived early at the train station. Twyla wasn't there, and Reg figured he had some waiting to do. He walked around for several blocks, feeling that people were gawking at him in his suede jacket and linen slacks. They didn't have a Dunsmuir store here. Meredith sashayed into the store, picked out what she wanted Reg to wear and had it delivered to their home. When she got tired of his apparel, she sent it to the Sally Ann and got him some more. She had lost all of her post- pregnancy weight and had gotten a tubal ligation. Twyla had had more difficulty with slimming down, but she was looking good. She and Willem might have another child, she said.

Reg wandered some more through downtown Mason River. He ended up in the public library but couldn't think of why. Then he headed back to the train station. She still wasn't there. Reg started to think that maybe Twyla wouldn't show up: she had broken a leg and couldn't dance, she had lost her nerve and just decided to stand him up. Mason River existed just as a place for dumb Canucks like himself to waste their time and money. He did something he wasn't supposed to do, and now he was paying for it.

On a bench outside the train station some men sat. Reg asked them if they knew where the Mason River Community Center was.

"There's supposed to be a dance performance there. My wife is in the dance troupe. I can't seem to find her."

"Lost your wife, eh?" said one of the men. "Now all you got left is your girlfriend." The men all laughed.

Reg wandered around some more, thinking maybe he should just head back to Bayporte. He was looking at the parking lot, to figure out which car was his, when he felt a tap on his shoulder. He turned around and smiled.

"Think I wasn't gonna make it?" asked Twyla, throwing her arms around his neck.

...

They had Chinese food in a restaurant next door to one of the hotels. Reg was so nervous that he had trouble holding his margarita steady.

"I suppose we could have found a better meeting

point than the train station," she said.

"Well, you're here now and so am I, and that's what matters."

"After we eat, you should check in. I'll join you a few minutes later. It looks better that way."

"Being bad feels pretty good," Reg told her. "I'm waiting for the good feeling to start. So far I've felt like the cheating husband." He added, "But I'm better now. Usually we talk on the phone. It's weird, to sit here and talk in person."

"Your anxiety is understandable," said Twyla. "Considering what we're up to. Sometimes being bad feels bad...at least at first."

They played kneesies under the table.

"I still want to see you dance," he said.

"Yes, fine." Twyla pouted a bit. Her upper lip was completely hairless; she had also plucked her eyebrows into a couple of super-fine arches. She looked as feminine now as she could, but still had some masculine handsomeness. She was so tall, too, and her shoulders had an annoying muscularity.

"The Mason River Community Center," she said. "I didn't know they had a community center here. Mason River is so small that you can cover it on foot in about fifteen minutes."

Reg grinned. "We'll have fun being bad."

Twyla smiled. Her teeth were incredibly white, and not perfectly straight, and her lips were naturally a bright pink, which contrasted well with her dark complexion.

"Just being bad," he said. "No big deal. Lots of

people do this. In some ways, what we're doing is a good thing for a marriage."

Twyla frowned. "Don't start rationalizing what we're doing. This is good for a marriage? The hell it is. We're cheating on our partners, period."

"I agree. We'll do this just once. It will be memorable. You said so yourself."

"Sometimes I say stupid things," Twyla said.

...

Not long after Willem flew somewhere to record something, Twyla phoned Reg and asked him to come over to babysit. She had errands to run and wanted to leave her daughter at home.

"I'm surprised you don't go over there and wipe her ass," Meredith said.

I probably would, he thought. He had helped her clean up a time or two during Willem's absences. Her home was a spectacular, imaginative mess: no dishwasher or laundry detergent, debris everywhere, dried food stains. While there, he played some of Willem's music and did their dishes and bought some detergent at the corner store. By the time Twyla got home, the place was in decent shape.

Twyla was cross. "I fought with my therapist this morning." Reg guessed that Twyla had started the fight. "She said I'm competing with my mother." Twyla said that Reg's insistence on cleaning up after other people was a power-grab. "Maybe you should see a shrink yourself."

Reg left soon after, and got mad at Twyla for speaking to him that way. He also got mad at himself for not defending himself against her, that bitchy slob.

...

Reg wasn't interested in Twyla's capacity for kind and thoughtful behavior. He wanted to be abused by her, and she was good at that. He watched her perform once and was fascinated by how she made sure she didn't look at him or in his direction.

He waited until a ridiculous hour, then called her hotel room.

"I was just thinking about you."

"That's nice." Pause. "That's nice, Wil."

He frowned. Did she have a roommate who might overhear, or did she actually think her husband was on the line?

"This is me. Reg."

"Yeah, I hear you, lover. Goodnight." Click.

...

Willem and Twyla have moved to Los Angeles. They are affluent now; Willem is now much in demand as a session musician, and he has already been nominated for a couple of Grammys. Twyla, much slimmer now, teaches dance classes at a community college. Her hair is now past her shoulders and streaked with blonde, to make her look younger and more feminine.

Their new house, built decades ago, is a salmon-colored Mediterranean that looks like dozens of others: red clay tiles cover its roof, arched entryways. Its pool is kidney shaped, its sauna is round. Willem swims every day, then sits in the sauna, because he fears aging, losing his vitality, being considered old and used up.

Reg flew down to see sometimes. His trips to Los Angeles became more frequent as his acting career progressed, and he liked to have someplace to stay where they knew his name. They liked to ask him about Bayporte. They said the longer they lived in America, the more Canadian they became.

One evening, as they sat enjoying the southern California sunset, Twyla told Reg a story about their daughter Danielle, who lived in their basement suite. Their other daughter, Nicole, had an apartment in the suburbs. Danielle entertained her boyfriends in the basement suite.

"I was trying to take a nap. Wil was out of town," Twyla said. I heard Dani downstairs crying out, *Yes, yes!* Well, if you fart down there, we can hear it up here. She knows that, and we thought she would mind her manners—"

"Not her. She doesn't care," interjected Willem.

"But Dani just said that if we didn't like the noise, we should turn up our TV set. So I just kept hearing her and wasn't sure what to do, since I had already asked her to pipe down and that didn't work. So I went down there and said I needed to get some things out of the storage room and I made as much noise as I could. Dani didn't care. I wish she would find her own place and take her horny boyfriends with her."

Reg told them about his divorce, Meredith's reluctant disclosure of her personal financial worth. She had remarried, to the scion of a mining company whose family was probably worth more than hers.

"I was poor and she was rich. Mixed marriages don't work," he told them.

"I wonder how her new husband likes those

clown figurines you were so fond of," Twyla said.

"I still like Meredith," said Reg.

"What? Why?" asked Twyla.

"Because she put up with me for all those years."

"Speaking of which," Twyla said, "Willem wants a divorce."

So they sat and drank beer and explored Willem's options. Did he want to stay married to Twyla, marry someone else or return to bachelorhood? Did he just want to be young again...?

"Oh, puh-leeze," Willem said. "Being young is overrated. What I'm going through is an existential crisis that probably started when I was three."

"He's been in California for too long," Twyla said. "He's open, free and liberated. He speaks his mind. He just puts it out there and says, 'There it is. Deal with it.'"

Twyla went to get a plate of things to nibble on. Reg and Willem took turns staring at the fireplace. She returned presently with a platter of cold cuts, cheese and crackers.

"His new candor?" she says. "He sees it as progress."

"Isn't it great?" asked Willem. "To freely admit my ambivalence about you and our marriage? I love you and hate you. I want to be with you always and never want to see you again. It's the human condition, but most of us are too chickenshit to deal with it."

"I'm too chickenshit to deal with it," Reg said.

"Then let's talk about something else," Willem

said.

"Good idea," Reg said. "This whole conversation is about Willem: What does he want or not want? Gotta keep Willem happy or he'll throw a temper tantrum."

"Fuckin'-A," said Twyla.

"And *you*"—Reg pointed at Twyla—"are not his momma, so how come you're acting like you are? When you cater to him the way you do, you enable his bad behavior. Tell your old man to shut up or fuck off. Don't take any more of his bullshit."

Twyla turned to Willem and, like an actor trying out a brand-new line, said, "Listen, you prick, I'm sick of you and your childish crap. Either grow up or get out."

"Reg said it's your fault, too. He said you've been *enabling* me," replied Willem.

"Well, what does Reg know? He's just some two-bit actor who couldn't keep his own marriage together," Twyla said.

"When you were in high school," Willem said, "you were sort of like Jesus with the lepers: 'I will be your friend if no one else will.' Therefore, you were surrounded by pariahs and you probably tried to cure them of whatever made them pariahs. You're still doing that, and you just make them feel that much worse about being pariahs."

"Then why did I hook up with you?" Twyla asked. "You're no pariah. You're gorgeous and talented. Your only problem is that you don't realize how fortunate you've been all your life."

"I was tempted to stop therapy, but my shrink said, 'You can't stop now! You're still weird!'" Willem said.

"Actually, your shrink said, 'You can't stop therapy now! My mortgage isn't paid off yet!'" Twyla said.

"Actually, my shrink is a fifteen-year-old whore down on Hollywood Boulevard. When not in jail, she's been most helpful in sorting out my issues," Willem said.

He got up and went into another room.

Reg watched him walk by. His T-shirt was emblazoned with the words THE OLDER I GET, THE BETTER I WAS. He was svelte, nearly emaciated. His gray hair was thick and curly. He had a chocolate-bronze tan. There seemed something very artificial and slick about him. Reg thought of Michael Jackson, minus the glitter glove.

"Wil is wasting away to nothing. Is he OK?"

"It's his new look: 'emaciated chic.'"

"You two must never divorce," Reg said, "because you would probably lose this beautiful house."

He lay back on the hooked rugs and looked at the white walls, white drapes, handmade furniture and abstract paintings. Far below them, but wonderfully visible through the huge living room window, was the spectacle of Sunset Boulevard traffic.

Twyla and Willem left Los Angeles for Toronto, then Montreal. They seemed to forget Sundown, and Reg had to tell them their old street address. When Reg lived in one place, he often thought of the others, and remembered them as being far better than they were. While in Prince Andrew, he thought often of Bayporte and the train station where Marge had worked. He also thought of rainy days when he drove over to the North Side with June in her raincoat, visiting with Twyla. He liked the tall trees and large empty spaces in that part of town; they were gone now, replaced with highrise condos and shopping malls. He fondly remembers the little stores and cedar dampness of Twyla and Willem's house. The freshness of air close to the sea. The young women looking out of front windows, older people walking dogs, everyone in sight glad to be there.

Other memories disturbed him.

He had felt despondent during the flight from Mason River. He felt close to tears as he sat in Bayporte International Airport. He was unable to overcome this feeling of despair and simply go home to Meredith. An RCMP officer sat down next to him and asked if there was something wrong. I must be making a fool of myself, Reg thought, for a cop to come by. I hope he won't Taser me.

He got up and walked to the airport bar, ordered a beer, then a second one. But he just felt sick then, and he wondered: What is my suffering about? It was useless, good for nothing, grief without a lesson. Masochism, as if he had whacked himself with a hammer. That's how he sees it sometimes; other times, he views it as natural and unavoidable, a series of beginnings and endings, the reason he is here at the airport instead of being in Meredith's house.

Meredith just stood and stared when Reg told her. She had no how-could-you scolding ready for him, she threw no temper tantrum, did not even shoot him a reproving look. As he spoke, and he spoke plenty, she stayed mute, as if he were speaking a foreign language and at some point would provide a translation.

He chose his words with care. He said only that he had had "an inappropriate relationship" with Twyla. Putting it that way made him congratulate himself on dressing up his indiscretion with a sort of dignity. It did nothing to assuage Meredith's grief; she stood there and looked at him as if he had just punched her in the stomach.

The telephone rang, and Reg picked it up, believing it was Twyla, who wanted to run away with him. Instead, it was someone from a casting agency, remembering Reg from Twyla's party and wondering if he was interested in auditioning for a part.

Not Twyla.

Reg wants his mind to shut off. He would rather not think about painful things; he wants to stare out at the sky, contemplate the stars, imagine what's really out there. The myriad problems of everyday life sometimes overwhelm him, so catatonia seems an attractive alternative. "I want to show you how I've been spending my money," Twyla tells Reg. "All that talk about living 'off the grid'? Well, forget it. We're buying stuff, too. Why not?

"Sony, Hitachi, BMW. Cappuccino makers, big-screen TVs. It's way too much fun. You know, it's not so bad, selling out. It has its good points."

…

On one occasion, they invited Reg to a party, he accepted, and he stayed long after everyone else left.

They all sat on the floor, stoned on Chablis. The party had been great fun, the place was a mess and none of them felt like cleaning up. Reg felt horny. Twyla said that parties were such fun, it was a shame they didn't have more of them.

"I've had enough to drink," Reg said. "What else is there to do?"

"Fuck," said Willem.

"I don't do men," Reg said.

"I had Twyla in mind."

"I don't want to watch you boff your wife."

"You boff her. I'll watch."

"I'm not into kink," said Reg. "Especially after all that wine."

"Do your best," Willem told him. Reg relented. He started to forget that Willem was there, despite the man's murmurs. Reg completed the act and enjoyed it more than not, though he felt as if he had ended up at a swingers' den and been included in some of their twisted fun. He woke up very early the next morning and left after getting dressed. He needed to get home; he felt angry at Willem and Twyla for taking advantage of him. When he felt exploited, he knew all he could do was get home and be by himself. He walked over to the nearest shopping mall and got into a taxi, promising himself he would never contact Twyla and Willem again. He also mentally wrote them a letter telling them how much they had disappointed him. He felt gratified by the eloquence of his letter and imagined how the blushes would burn his readers' cheeks as they read his prose. But that was all he did: he wrote the letter in his mind, and forgot about it by the time the taxi deposited him at his house. Reg made a point of keeping Willem and Twyla as friends. Reg knew how many friends and acquaintances he had—he had few of the former, many of the latter—and knew that friends were harder to find, the older you got. At least for him they were.

Right Place, Right Time

Reg dreamed about June after he had moved out and wondered what would become of their relationship. They met while walking up a hill. June was dressed all in white and a mysterious, hushed music followed her. When they were close enough to hear each other, Reg asked, "Which of us do you want to stay with, Mummy or me?" June didn't answer the question; she just said, "Why don't we all stay together and pretend...?" Reg had gotten a broadcasting job in a northern city.

June lay in the bed where her parents used to sleep. When that happened, Reg and Meredith found other places to sleep, such as June's bed or the big sofa in the den. No one was sure where to sleep from one night to the next. Reg began packing his suitcases when nobody else was around. He spent his evenings in an insolated part of the house, watching TV. One time, he went into the living room and discovered Meredith dusting framed pictures of them. He got mad. He moved closer and saw one of the pictures, of the two of them at Northup, when they were dating. Now Reg pointed at it.

"That was a lie," he said. "We were doomed, even then."

Meredith nodded. Even on their wedding day, Reg knew their divorce was inevitable. When June was born, he wondered which of them would get custody of her.

"No sense in dwelling on it," Meredith said.

Reg blamed himself for letting their marriage deteriorate, even if he knew it wasn't entirely his fault. He hadn't tried to hasten its demise, although he knew their end was coming. You can't stop the inevitable, you can only prepare for it.

"Where do you want to live?" he asked June, sounding as gentle as he could. Instead of speaking, the child pointed at Meredith.

"You don't have to go, Daddy" June said. "You don't fight any more." Meredith looked at Reg. The child was right: her parents did not fight any more. They had had fistfights in the kitchen and living room; Meredith had kicked Reg in the scrotum, and he had sent her sprawling against the leaded-glass back door. But to June, fighting parents were better than none at all.

He emailed Tammy, telling her his plans. She was a drama instructor at the University of Edmonton, and they had met in Bayporte a couple of years earlier, when they did a couple of radio commercials together. Reg was deeply infatuated with her. They swapped emails and always agreed to try to see each other. When she learned of Reg's separation, he was afraid that Tammy might not want anything more to do with him, but that was not the case. Tammy seemed indifferent.

Reg told people that his breakup with Meredith had nothing to do with Tammy or anyone else. Still, he had chosen to take the broadcasting job up there in Prince Andrew because it seemed like the right thing to do.

June smiled and said goodbye to him. She wanted to stay in Bayporte, in her own school, with her own friends.

She waved at them.

"Goodbye! Good luck!"

Reg pictured himself moving out of Meredith's house and into a furnished room in Old Town, a decrepit, seedy section of downtown Bayporte. Old Town was lined with hotels featuring bathrooms down the hall and soiled women in the downstairs pub. Reg would not have much to do all day but sit and ask himself: What's next? He would not mind escaping the anal-retentive cleanliness of Meredith's neighborhood, and he could probably even get used to the austerely simple existence of sleeping on the floor, if it came to that. But, instead, he took the radio job in Prince Andrew, a small northern city where he would read the news, clean the bathrooms and think up story ideas.

He moved into a two-bedroom apartment as clean and boring as a Holiday Inn. Prince Andrew was a small city rather than a town. Tammy said she wanted to see him when the next conference happened in his region. But she called later and said she couldn't do it, their get-together would have to wait.

Reg's colleague Shannon asked him if he was at all suspicious of what Tammy had said. Reg said he was above considering anyone suspicious, and maybe that was his problem.

"You were married to the Dunsmuir girl, right?"

Shannon asked. She did a not-for-women-only show thrice each week and frequently talked to feminists' groups. She and Reg became friends because Shannon always befriended the newcomer to the station. She had a boyfriend in Bayporte and suspected him of cheating on her.

"Men do that," she said as they sat in the Tim Horton's doughnut shop across the street from the station. "Men have pricks. They *are* pricks. No offense."

She told Reg about the owner of the radio station, who owned half the small-market stations in western Canada. He began having an affair with Shannon and gave her a gold Rolex for her birthday. "When I took it in to be appraised, the jeweler said it was a fake. My Timex is worth more than this Rolex." Reg thought Shannon looked fake, too, with her badly bleached blonde hair and poorly made up face. In Bayporte, they would have thought she was a whore on her way to pick up trade at the TransCanada Railway Station.

At Christmas, Reg visited Bayporte and stayed at Meredith's house. June seemed to have grown; she was exuberant and sinewy, full of cartwheels and giggles. They took long walks together along the dry sidewalks. There wasn't a trace of snow.

"I'm at school and suddenly I realize that you're gone," June said.

"I'm not dead. I've just moved away."

"You're not here. That's as bad as dead."

Reg said he would take her with him when he went back to Prince Andrew. Meredith just shrugged and said to go ahead, you can always bring her back if it doesn't work out. Reg packed a suitcase for June. Later, the child said she thought he was just bluffing, or trying to provoke Meredith, by taking June away.

The northbound train went very slowly, stopping at every little station to let passengers on and off. Reg and June made it fun, getting off and clowning around on the platform.

"Oh, God! It's so cold!" June jumped up and down, crying out, smiling and hugging herself. Outside, the scenery was a vision of gray-and-green loveliness.

"We'll have to get you some winter gear." Reg assumed she knew that she was moving up there with him, not merely visiting.

Back on board, June sank into a deep slumber while Reg stared out into the darkness, content as the train rumbled on and the snow fell in fat chunks. He liked this slow pace of travel.

They reached Prince Andrew, and June soon started school. She became popular with her classmates, and within a couple of weeks was bringing her friends home or going to visit them. Reg did all the shopping and laundry. They had no housekeeper now, no staff or money to provide every possible convenience. His radio job was challenging and difficult, and his many household chores wore him out. But he no longer felt like Mr. Meredith Dunsmuir, freeloader.

He bought June a laptop computer and a color TV. He met her at school one day and saw that she had been crying.

"Today I heard someone calling out for Davey

and I thought it was *my* Davey." Davey had been her favorite playmate at school in Bayporte.

"We'll just have to get you a new Davey," Reg said.

"It wouldn't be the same," she said.

"Well, let's go get something to eat."

The weather was dreadful that day. The sky looked like iron and the wind was icy. Some of the ice and snow had melted, then froze again, so Reg felt as if he were walking on an ice rink. Around them, boys and girls, just out of school, whooped and hollered, sliding along on the ice, not caring if they collided with each other. They annoyed Reg as much as the skateboard pests in downtown Bayporte.

All June wanted was a chocolate milkshake. They

went into Buddy's, a 1950s-style hangout with a jukebox and neon signs.

"This place will be gone soon," Reg said as they settled into a booth. "They'll turn it into a White Spot or Denny's."

"You didn't love Mummy. That's why you left. That's what Mummy says."

"Your mum is a fine woman." He was prepared for that from his daughter. "Sometimes people can have very deep feelings for each other but they find they can't live together or stay married to each other."

June made a face. "I don't believe that. You just didn't love her enough."

Well, kid, if that's what you want to believe, I can't talk you out of it. To him, the words *like, enough* and even *love* seemed too small for Meredith Dunsmuir.

"I don't want this," June said, pushing her milkshake away. "Let's go buy a puppy."

They went to the shopping mall and bought a toy poodle they named Charlee. They also got an armload of puppy food and toys. At home, June loved to watch the TV talk shows like *Geraldo* and *Jerry Springer*, especially if they had themes such as "I Had a Child with My Brother's Wife." Reg let her watch them even during dinner because they kept her so quiet. He had to make food and store it in plastic tubs in the freezer. After that, he would have to enter into the usual negotiations to get June to take her bath and go to bed. At the end of the evening, Reg could sit with a cold beer and feel proud that he'd managed for another day. He thought of a TV talk show theme:

Could Meredith Have Done Nearly As Well As a Single Parent?

Did June think she and he were just playing a game by moving up here together? If so, was she right? Daddy Moved Away and Took Me with Him. Back in Bayporte, there was enough of everything to keep her happy for any number of lifetimes, so whenever June tired of hiding out in the boonies, Reg could always put her on the next flight back to Bayporte.

"Why did you get divorced?" Shannon asked him. "I've been there and done that, too."

Reg wondered why people asked such questions, when there were too many answers and most of the answers were nobody's business. Domestic violence, misplaced priorities, infidelity...

"Frustration," said Shannon. "That's my reason. Being with the same person, having the same conversations...I just got totally frustrated."

Reg laughed. "Well, that's a new reason, and an honest one. It's better than 'irreconcilable differences.'"

"We had those, too. And infidelity. I was carrying on with this other guy who traveled a lot. He wrote to me overseas, saying how much I meant to him. I was so moved by this that I looted my bank account and went over there to be with him. I really pursued him. Today I believe they call it 'stalking.'"

"Did you catch up with him?"

"No. He kept going and I ran out of money. I had just enough cash to get back home, so that's what I did." She paused. "A few years later I bumped into him somewhere. He was all, 'Gee, it's too bad we couldn't get together overseas.' I told him it was OK, I had a nice time anyway. The truth was, I was still paying the bills from going overseas to hook up with him."

At the radio station, Reg did a variety of things, from updating their mailing lists to making coffee, and he spent much of his time on story ideas. He came up with a direction for the station to take: cover Prince Andrew as a northern hub of scientific and technological innovation. He went to the local college and interviewed the professors. He went back to the station and presented his work to his bosses, and they laughed at him. The station had been doing that sort of story for a couple of years already.

He thought of Tammy, often. He called and sent her amorous emails; they made plans to see each other. Without the presence of her in his life, he would have felt like an aging divorced man, sad and pathetic. Reg decided to attend the next broadcasting conference, in Calgary, and he told Tammy he hoped to see her then. They were giddy on the phone, like girls planning a slumber party. He had one of his neighbors move in to look after June while he was in Calgary. He would need to take a bus for an hour to reach the nearest puny airport, then fly in a plane that looked scarcely more aerodynamic than a child's toy. He imagined going up in such an aircraft and crashing somewhere in the mountains, then dying or surviving, eating or being eaten by another passenger. The prospect of a liaison with Tammy seemed worth the risk. He felt so exhilarated that he played with June, listened as she talked about whatever she seemed interested in.

"I don't *feel* good," the girl said, almost in tears. He checked her temperature: over a hundred. Her skin was clammy. Reg couldn't call Tammy at work or home, but he did cancel the taxi and knew he couldn't go away the next morning, even if June did feel better.

The next morning, with June bundled up and chuckling at kiddie shows on TV, Reg called Tammy. "Wow! You're here!" she exclaimed.

He said, "Not exactly..."

June's cough persisted. Reg discovered that he couldn't seem to warm up the apartment adequately. He called the caretaker, who said to expect him when they saw him. Reg threatened him with doing a radio program on negligent caretakers if he didn't get better service. The caretaker came up promptly, made some adjustments and restored the heat. Reg thanked him and sighed with satisfaction, as if he were a slum-dweller who had threatened to kick some ass if his social worker didn't make sure the check arrived on time. Nobody had told Reg that you couldn't threaten a social worker because it would accomplish nothing. When he lived in Meredith's house, heat seldom failed to come on, and when it did fail, all you had to do was snap your fingers and someone immediately appeared to fix it.

By the time Reg returned to work, June was feeling better. Still, he was wracked with anxiety. When he came home, he found that June was sitting up in bed, wide awake, eager to talk about the nonsense she had watched on TV all day.

Reg and Tammy said little about their mutual disappointment. They called each other fewer times but sent affectionate emails. Tammy called him to say that her children were going overseas for a month and she would be joining them, but before she departed she would be able to spend a dozen days with him. A dozen days! She said he should fly out to see her; she would be really happy. He said he would start on the arrangements. He could probably get someone to look after June easily.

Tammy sounded happy. She suggested that the two of them travel to Jasper, a popular ski resort. Could they spend three days there, even four? Reg agreed, but he still got depressed and anxious when his travel plans were changed, especially by someone else. He was to leave on a Friday, and his bus trip and the airport he would go to were the same. They got out their calendars and decided on specific days for their liaison. He decided a weekend would be best and he could throw in a Friday and Monday, too. Shannon would do whatever needed to be done. Shannon owed him, after all, from the times Shannon was too hung over to come in and Reg had done her work in addition to his own.

He had a couple of weeks to make the arrangements to see Tammy. One of his neighbors agreed to stay with June while Reg was out of town. He hoped Tammy wouldn't expect him to ski. *Am I the only Canadian who can't ski?* He was a competent ice skater; maybe they could do that. They would certainly spend most of their time talking, drinking and having sex. On the phone, they were polite to each other, almost boring. He couldn't remember that clearly how she looked; he had some nagging visions of her as being short and chunky, with graying hair and a lined face. But he was unable to recall any really unacceptable quality about her, no hairy armpits or foul smells. What he could remember was getting together with her, and coming away with the feeling that their time together had been somehow unsuccessful. That feeling made him especially eager to see her again and show her how much fun he could be.

He finalized his plans: leave Friday morning and take the same bus and plane he'd been going to use the last time.

A few days before he was to leave, the snow began to fall in Prince Andrew. Reg didn't worry; it seemed to melt as soon as it landed. He wondered if it would snow in Jasper. Snow could be a pretty sight, in the right place, especially if *you* were in the right place, too, such as inside a heated hotel room, with the right person, in a big bed. After making love, you could watch the snow fall. The snow in Prince Andrew fell continuously for two days, and when Reg went to the travel agency to get his ticket, the agent told him that the airport was closed due to inclement weather. Reg told himself that was OK; he didn't want to fly anyway, especially in bad weather. He decided he wanted to take the train instead, although of course it didn't go directly to Jasper, it went halfway around Canadian before it got to where he wanted to go. I'll take the bus, he said. The agent called to make sure that the buses were running. Reg began to panic, thinking of a long bus ride through the snow, having to share a toilet with people he didn't know.

"The bus departs after midnight and gets into Jasper in the afternoon," the ticket agent said.

"Let's do it," Reg said.

"You must be some kind of skiing enthusiast,"

the ticket agent said.

"It's what I live for." He wondered how many other people had gone to such trouble just to get laid.

He went home and decided the bus was better than no Tammy at all. He would just have to ask his neighbor to move in that night. The neighbor was already there, playing games with June.

"I'm sorry," the neighbor said, "but I can't stay."

She went on to explain that there was some sort of family emergency down in Bayporte and they needed her there. Reg didn't listen; he was an experienced actor and a proficient liar himself, and her story sounded as hollow as a balloon. He started calling other people who might be available, people who knew people who might be available. No luck. Reg hung up the phone and stared at it for the longest time.

"Maybe," June said, "I could do OK here by myself for a few days."

"Nice try."

"I've done it before. I'm not a baby, Daddy."

Reg snapped his fingers. "I have an idea." He turned to the girl. "How would you like to come with me?"

June beamed. "Let's do it!" They hurried about the apartment, packing a big suitcase with clothes and coloring books. Reg did not stop to think about what June would do once they got to Jasper, or how he would pay for an extra room (assuming there was one). June was thrilled not to be left alone with a sitter. She seemed to think of the long bus ride as an adventure. Reg remembered to call for a taxi well before midnight.

The taxi inched its way through the streets of Prince Andrew and at times seemed to get stuck in the ice and snow. The bus station was not a station at all, but located in the corner of a popular casino. Reg liked that just fine. He thought Bayporte's bus station, located at the TransCanada Railway Station, was a dreary and dangerous place, and some bus stations in major American cities were even more forbidding. Reg left June just inside the casino's entrance with their luggage and went to the ticket window. When he returned, she was dozing, her chin nearly touching her chest.

"Wake up, sleepy head," Reg said.

She looked up at him. "I was just resting my

eyes."

"You can sleep all you want once we're on the bus."

Reg hoped she would drop off to sleep and stay that way all night. He wondered if the bus would be as toasty warm as this casino was, or if he should have brought a blanket along with everything else. Still, he didn't want to think of arriving at their destination, smelly, cranky and impotent, dragging along half of everything they owned.

Some other people waited for the bus, too. A couple in jeans and sweatshirts, carrying backpacks and looking underfed and overtired, as if they had spent the past few years hiking overseas. A chubby, white-haired old woman wearing a toque. A Pakistani or Indian woman with a small child. A youngish man on a bench not far from June; he looked drunk or stoned. Reg hoped he was just sitting there because it was warm in the casino; he didn't want to share the bus with a drunk who might puke. He also thought June should use the toilet in the casino before they boarded the bus. June was walking around, looking at the slot machines and flashing lights. Reg was sure there was an age restriction here and that a security guard would soon come by and ask the little girl who, and where, her mother or father was. Reg thought maybe he should buy some sandwiches and fruit juice to take with them on the bus; if he didn't, he probably would regret it soon.

Suddenly he heard an announcement over the public address system. "All buses canceled due to bad weather."

Reg hurried over to the window and demanded to

know what was happening and couldn't something be done about it?

The man sighed and said, "The news just came in. The highways are closed, so no buses will be coming in or going out tonight."

Reg nodded and took a deep breath. "What other travel options do I have?"

The man frowned. "I'm not sure what you mean."

"Well, there are trains, planes..."

"Sir, nothing is available. It's a Canadian winter, you know. These things happen."

Reg turned away and saw June over by the slot machines. The child loved the music, sound effects and lights.

June hurried over to him and pulled him to the

side. "Look what I found." She opened her hand and showed him a wad of bills: hundreds, fifties, twenties. She swallowed hard and made a shushing noise, her face florid and sweaty.

"Put that in your pocket," Reg commanded. "We're going home."

The child nodded and they hustled out to the same taxi they had exited minutes earlier. June patted her bulging pocket, as if to make sure her money was still there.

When they got home, Reg opened himself a can of beer. June headed straight for the dinner table and took out the wad of money from the casino. She separated the bills by color.

"This is awesome!" she said. "Just awesome!" She spoke in a queerly adult, mature voice. Her father had never heard her sound that way; she sounded the way a grown-up would after having gotten a lot of money for nothing. He felt disturbed.

"People get careless in casinos," he said. "They go in there with all that money and get so carried away that they don't bother to make sure they've put their money away."

"We don't have to return it, do we?" June asked, as if she were a bank robber or some other kind of thief. Reg got the feeling that June saw this bit of good luck as something that must somehow be illegal, or at least unethical. She was old enough to know that money didn't grow on trees, nor did it sit in fat little bundles on casino carpets. Something was wrong here, but why did it feel so right?

Reg laughed as June, intoxicated by the sight of

red fifties here, green twenties there and brown hundreds off to the side, couldn't think straight enough to count it all. He laughed at how this thick roll of money, found by a small child in a gambling joint, could be seen as compensation for the disappointments they'd endured over the past few days. Also, it was the kid's money, not his. He didn't want it. They played with it and threw it at each other. This was one of the few nights in which Reg felt like a father with a child, able to put aside the pressures of everyday life and just enjoy June's company. He wondered how long this good feeling would last.

Tammy sent him a long, loving, oh-well email about how they had underestimated the fury of Canadian winter. She was heading overseas with her family soon, and hoped she and Reg might be able to get together at some point. Reg wrote back that he would look forward to it...whenever.

The weather grew milder; the snow melted fast and Reg at times felt as if he were back in Bayporte, city of eternal rain. Meredith emailed him, asking if Reg agreed it was time to send June home. She said he could put her on a flight back to Bayporte and ship her belongings down through the post office or the bus service, whichever would be more convenient for him.

Wouldn't that be better, Meredith asked, for a little girl, instead of following along wherever the wind happened to blow her free-spirited father...? Wasn't it paramount to do whatever was best for the child...?

Reg wanted very much to claim that he had made a perfectly acceptable life for himself and June, but how truthful was that? Meredith was right, as usual. Reg was getting frustrated with Prince Andrew, with its modest opportunities, ignorant people and cold weather. His pay was poor and his career could stagnate indefinitely. Why not move to Toronto, with its big population and greater opportunities? He and June could explore eastern Canada together. Or would he and she just stay in a series of hotels and apartments while Reg tried to resume his career? And if Toronto didn't work out, what then? Would they just take off to Montreal or some other part of Canada?

As much as Reg wanted to bum around with June, even he conceded that the child came first. So he put June on a flight back home. Meredith immediately got her involved in horseback riding, tennis and gymnastics, to keep her busy and physically fit. They sent Reg a picture of June holding Charlee and beaming. He packed her possessions into a couple of suitcases and sent them down via bus courier.

He found a couple of unsent emails that June had sent:

"Davey, have you found a new best friend yet? I hope not."

"Mummy, have you found a new husband yet? I hope not."

GEORGE ONSTOT

Sophie's Choice

Reg, still feeling lonely, sometimes walks through the streets of Bayporte, a longtime resident who feels at times like a newcomer. On Roberts or Grand Street, he sees people in nightclubs, restaurants, stores and apartments. Neon signs, bobbing heads and merry voices. Saturday-night parties, Sunday dinners. Everyone seems to know each other. He wishes someone would ask him in so he could check things out, even if he believes boredom would drive him back out again soon. Reg wants to party; he doesn't care where, he'd be happy in some kid's cramped basement apartment where they're all a dozen years his junior and cannabis resin litters the carpets and all the mismatched dishes and cups have chips and cracks. He might even like a dingy room where they blare the music and worship the Che Guevara and Charles Manson posters on the wall.

Of course, Reg would rather drink imported beer with chic people under high ceilings. He is a professional actor, able to work all rooms, mingle with all crowds.

He does go to parties, sometimes. Recently, he attended a gathering in a highrise downtown, overlooking the river. Reg had bought a small house in the suburbs and taught theatre at a community college. His friends thought him strange to move into such a humble home, considering he had just divorced one of the richest women in town. But the lawyers and accountants had shaken him down, so he taught acting. He did act, when he could; alas, his screen royalties amounted to chump change.

He had driven a long distance to that party, and had done so out of loneliness. His host, too, had probably invited him because Reg didn't do nearly enough partying. As soon as he arrived, the hostess took him into the bedroom so he could take off his coat. On the bed, a poodle suckled her puppies.

"Cute," said Reg.

"I know. They're purebred. When they get bigger, we're going to sell them." She bent over and started baby-talking the dog and making smooching noises. The dog just stared at her. Reg saw a wall mirror in the bedroom, about six feet wide, in which he and the hostess were visible. He didn't like looking in mirrors while standing next to people much younger than himself. He was wearing black shirt and matching slacks, which made him look like an aging man who wished to appear younger. In a party like this, others would be the center of attention and the guests would likely ignore him. He would be just another fringe guest, a piece of human furniture. They might want to rest their drinks on him.

In the living room, he drank beer and told a story. He'd had a cat, and the pet jumped or fell from his highrise apartment.

"I hate to admit it, but I was just as glad to see him gone. Can you imagine not liking your own cat? I've heard that cats can survive big falls, but I think this one was a goner."

His audience laughed, even though the story wasn't especially funny. The teller mattered, not the tale, and Reg was an entertaining raconteur. His story made them laugh, or maybe it was mainly his delivery and body language, and those who didn't listen looked bemused, as if they'd missed the punch line.

"I looked all around the apartment, but the cat wasn't there," he added.

"The hazards of highrise life," said the man standing next to him. He was a professor at Northup, someone Reg had known for some time if superficially. "There are worse dangers when you're on the higher floors." He pumped his hand in a masturbatory manner and everyone laughed because they all knew the news item: a city highrise onanist, indulging himself with the blinds open, had been spotted by neighbors and reported to the police, who entered the highrise and arrested him.

"They said his full name on the air and everything. Talk about public humiliation!"

"Your cat fell off the balcony," said the hostess in a disturbed sort of dreaminess. "I'm surprised you came here tonight. It takes time to grieve."

"Oh, it didn't happen recently." Reg, in truth, wasn't sure if it had happened at all.

"You were glad to get rid of the little fucker," said a tall redheaded girl Reg hadn't noticed before. "You should get another cat and throw it off the balcony, too. You can make it your new hobby."

Reg frowned. He recognized her as a student or alumna. After a few moments of mental groping, he remembered her name. "Heather," he said. "Nice to see you again. Heather. How have you been? Or need I ask?"

"Kill your pets, kill them dead," she half-chanted like a drunken hip-hop singer.

"Excuse me?" Reg tried to sound amused and provoked, goaded, the way a TV talk show host might indulge a bratty but celebrated young guest. At this party, of course, the expectation of good manners persisted; everyone surely wanted Reg to put Heather down with some wonderfully clever retort.

"Excuse *you*," said Heather to Reg. "There *is* no excuse for you, Reggie." She was freckled, sweating profusely and about-to-topple-over drunk. She had probably grown up in a home where people minded their manners and said little of what they thought, and now she was on her own, acting out as she pleased.

A sturdy, tall woman with dark wavy hair eased along and grabbed Heather by the arm. "Party's over.

You've had your fun." The woman hustled Heather out of the room.

"What do you suppose possessed her?" Reg asked. "Maybe she *was* possessed."

"Alienated, disaffected youth," said the man standing next to him. "It's not a new thing."

The hostess appeared and said, "Sorry, Reg. I didn't invite her. I don't know how she crashed this party."

He shook his head. "Heather was a student of mine." He really couldn't remember much else. The others were looking at him as if he had lots more to say about her.

"Was she one of those drama majors?" asked the man next to him. "That figures. All the young ones want to act on the screen. They see no-talent assholes winning Oscars and they get their little hearts set on fame and glitz."

Reg nodded. "What a troubled kid."

"Most children are. Then they take acting classes and call themselves 'emotional athletes.' They think acting is about wallowing in self-pity. They want to turn their classes into therapy groups, complain about their parents and seduce their teachers. Or have their teachers seduce *them*."

The tall, sturdy woman came back into the room and smiled at Reg, then slipped away. He shrugged and drank more beer, almost wishing that Heather had been an unstable, gifted young thespian he'd sexually exploited, then flunked. But she'd simply materialized from the room's stuffy air to snap at him.

He could not recall doing anything that might have enraged her. Some instructors yelled at students, used caretaker speech or ignored them. Not Reg. He was always tactful, diplomatic, eager to help and please.

A woman approached him and said, "I'm doing a paper on the relationship between mental illness and creativity." She added that she had seen Reg on TV many times and was eager to speak to him. She mentioned the names of many celebrities who had opened up about their mental issues. He thought that she—scrawny, intense, fidgety—looked like someone who'd battled plenty of her own demons.

"I suddenly feel hungry," Reg said.

"Then let's go into the kitchen," said the woman.

"I'm not creative or crazy," Reg said.

"Oh, I wouldn't say that."

Reg laughed.

The hostess had made chicken nuggets and a variety of other hot finger foods that made you thirsty. In the kitchen, some Northup faculty sat, leaned and laughed. Reg thought they looked young enough to be graduate students. Northup paid its professors well and liked them youthful, forward-thinking and highly practical. The U. coddled its scientists and engineers and neglected its humanities instructors. He smiled, and they looked away. Reg thought they were talking about him and Heather. He turned to the woman writing the paper about mentally ill people.

"You should eat a little something. It's really delicious."

"I'm not hungry," she replied.

Maybe that's your problem, he felt like saying. He figured out, quickly enough, that this woman attended the party because she knew she would have a few minutes alone with Reg.

"There's nothing wrong with *your* appetite," she said as he heaped chicken nuggets onto a small plate.

"There's nothing wrong with me, period."

He meant that as a joke but winced at how obnoxious he sounded. Also, he was not particularly hungry, just disappointed at how these people were refusing to eat all this delicious food. His problem right now was anxiety over his confrontation with Heather. He stood there in the kitchen, convinced he was the subject of derisive conversation.

Idiotic artsy-fartsy asshole.

Reg swore he heard someone say that of him. They were taking turns shooting ugly looks at him but he could not be absolutely sure of it. *Artsy-fartsy.* Was Reg that? He guessed he was. After all, hadn't he taken a position as a drama instructor when the acting jobs stopped happening? And hadn't he gotten the instructing job mainly because of his experience? He had only a bachelor's degree, while everyone else seemed to have a master's. For some peculiar reason, June floated into his mind just then. His daughter had her mother's voluptuousness, shiny blonde hair and big sunny smile. She wore a heavy gold chain around her neck. He couldn't find himself anywhere in her. She was a Dunsmuir; she played tennis, swam and rode horses with consummate seriousness and had her mother's gift for never failing or falling. When

Meredith suggested that her daughter get into organized sports, June said, "But that's competitive."

And what was wrong with that? Meredith wanted to know.

"Competition is pointless," June said, "because I would always win."

June Dunsmuir. Meredith Dunsmuir. Reg's women had refused his last name. That was OK. Reg wanted to become a Dunsmuir himself, so they would all have something in common. Too late now.

The dark-haired woman who'd gotten rid of Heather stood in the doorway, staring straight ahead, at no one in particular.

"Who's the woman who handled the troublemaker?" Reg asked the woman who was writing the paper.

"Her name is Sophie. She teaches at Northup. Humanities or something. I think she's had a couple of careers already."

"My kind of woman." Reg made eye contact with Sophie and gave her his biggest smile. As discouraged as he felt, he was beginning to feel warmer currents of energy, better vibrations.

If this woman smiles back, I will forgive Heather for trying to fuck up my evening.

Sophia returned his big open smile.

"This is a party," said the professor's wife, "not a singles' bar."

...

"So she said, 'This is a party, not a singles' bar.'"

Reg and Sophie laughed. They lay in Reg's bed, in his aging suburban house. The party had ended a few hours earlier. The month was May but felt like February. His house was chilled, and the heating system couldn't seem to be poked or prodded into generating sufficient warmth.

Sophie checked it out. "You definitely should invest in upgrades."

"I know, but I don't have time. Usually I just bring someone in and pay them to do it for me."

Sophie mentioned a few ways of generating heat: wood stoves, insulation. She got out of bed and started walking around, patting the walls.

"Don't do that right now. Come back to bed. You're making me cold."

"Think warm thoughts."

"Do you remember that girl? Heather, from the party?" Reg asked. "She wanted to apply for a grant, so she had come to me for help with it. She wanted to become the next Canadian superstar. That's what our confrontation at the party was about."

"You turned her down," Sophie said.

"No. I completely cooperated with her." Reg helped everyone as much as possible, when it came to getting students money for school.

He believed that every student should get every kind of financial aid, period.

"I guess she didn't get any money, so she was pissed off at me about it."

"If they turned her down, they probably had their

reasons," Sophie called from outside the bedroom. "It wasn't *your* fault."

"I know, but still..."

"There's not enough of *anything* to go around, Reg, so we all have to make do with what we have, or we just do without. Heather just thought she could have her own way with everyone and bully people when she didn't get things she wanted. The world is a competitive place and there were other applicants who deserved more financial aid than she did." Then, "You need a professional to come in here and outfit your house for winter."

"But what about her hatred? Her attitude? All that just from having been turned down for money?"

Sophie appeared in the doorway, nude. She was tall, perhaps six feet, and muscular. She put her hands on her head, as if for a breast exam. Reg liked her long, shiny, kinky black hair, smooth underarms, pierced nipples.

"What about Heather and her attitude? Enough of that. Let's talk about me. I'm this chick you picked up at a party and took home for the night. And right now, I'm a very *hungry* chick."

At the neighborhood mall Reg bought fresh gourmet coffee, eggs, cheddar cheese, shrimp and cream. He was in the throes of happiness that seemed effortless and eternal; he would probably have said that his fine mood was due to the blustery wind and painfully sunny sky rather than anything having to do with Sophie. At the mall, he also went in to see Black Lady, the psychic. Only her clothes were black; she was pallid, with silver hair.

"You look happy," she said.

"I have more happiness than I can stand," he said.

"Then you should bottle it and sell it. You'd make a million dollars."

. . .

Sophie cooked a feast with the ingredients from Reg's trip to the mall. Reg sat at the dinner table and watched her cook.

"I came from Sundown," he said. "I grew up with the idea that Sundown was this hick town for people who couldn't make it in the big city. I also thought my goal should be to get a good education and escape Sundown forever. So I studied like hell and got a scholarship to Northup, and when I moved here, I really learned about being a starving student. God, what an experience! I started to envy the people back in Sundown. And after I hooked up with Meredith, I learned that the rich people have problems, too. Everyone's screwed."

Sophie laughed. "You're screwed if you believe that money will make you happy. You could be happy here, you know, in this little house. You just need to fix it up a bit."

"I've told myself that many times. I just can't seem to get around to it. You should buy yourself a car."

Sophie usually took the bus. They had driven to Reg's house in his car.

"I'm a humble woman. I can use public transportation or just walk."

"Bad idea," Reg said. "If you take the bus, by the time you get to the campus, you'll be exhausted. You'll fall asleep in front of your students."

"If I got that tired, I'd just call in sick."

"I'm glad you came here with me," Reg said. "If you weren't here, I would start obsessing over that little bitch Heather. I hate confrontations. It's just one of my neuroses."

"That thing with Heather wasn't worth dick. In the grand scheme of things, that really was nothing."

"I've been this way for most of my life," he said.

"You can change your ways, if you're willing to work at it."

Before she left, Sophie drew up a list of things for Reg to do, mostly involving household maintenance.

"You should also start a garden. I'll help you with that, too."

Reg hugged her and said, "Sophie, you crazy cunt! Where have you been all my life?"

. . .

On Wednesday or Thursday, he went to the mall to see Black Lady. She said, "You've met someone special. A woman."

"I believe you're right."

"Big changes are in store for you. *Very* big changes."

Reg nodded. "Yes, yes. Good changes, I assume."

Black Lady shrugged. "We'll see."

He wasn't clear on what plans he and Sophie had

made, but he always expected her on the weekends and thought it best to have groceries in the house, so he went out and did some shopping. On Friday, he cleaned up and put fresh sheets on the bed, then made the initial preparations for dinner. He waited, and soon the doorbell rang. He wondered why she didn't invest in a car; the closest bus stop was several blocks away.

...

"Hate to bother you," said Black Lady. "I just wanted someone to talk to. Am I interrupting something?"

"Well, yes." Reg was breathing hard from rushing to open the door and half-expected Sophie to jump out from the bushes and say, "Surprise! Fooled ya, hey?"

"You don't know what's happening with her,"

Black Lady observed.

"No."

She looked up. "Raining again."

"You're the psychic. Make it stop."

Black Lady laughed, and Reg felt obligated to ask her in. Should he open the bottle of wine and offer her some? Black Lady might get drunk and give him a free session. But did she have anything to say that he wished to hear? Reg believed that Black Lady possessed some sort of mystical powers and was more than just an observant, clever hustler. She and Reg had spoken often, and he had come to consider her a friend of sorts (he used the word *friend* carefully and preferred *acquaintance*). But he wasn't being especially friendly at this moment with this woman, and it would have been the same with anyone but

Sophie. Everyone else was a nuisance.

"Want a cup of coffee?" he asked, thinking that Black Lady would give him a free session.

"The spirits are stingy tonight," she said. "I can't find her tonight."

"What are you talking about?"

"Sophie. I'm talking about her. I just don't see her in your future. I may be wrong, but I doubt it."

"Well, girlfriends come and go. They're liked buses. There's another one every fifteen minutes.

"Do you have anything of hers I could touch? Sometimes it helps me find the person's vibrations."

"Nope. She took her pink panties with her."

Hours after Black Lady left, Reg sat up, alone. The

sky grew darker The rain came down harder. He stared at the TV with the sound off. then looked at the clock. Nearly three in the morning. He grinned at how the TV, with its endless nonsense, could help a person through the night. He turned off the lights and TV because he didn't want anyone to see that he was still up. He crawled into bed but lay there sleepless. Then he got up, made coffee and sat in the kitchen. For several minutes he stared out the window. Sophie's somewhere out there. He wondered why she took the bus instead of driving a car. He wondered why he was living in an aging little house in the suburbs when, not long before, he was living with Meredith Dunsmuir. When he was with Meredith, he hated her and her big fancy house; now that he was away from her, which was what he wanted (or at least what he told himself he wanted), he wondered occasionally if he had made the right decision. Then there was Sophie, with whom he had dived into a relationship, and on whom he depended for his personal happiness. Had he not learned anything from his previous relationships? Would he ever learn any of the lessons that life routinely presented to him?

He blamed the wine on his low spirits. He wasn't a drinker; he was hypersensitive to the effects of depressants and stimulants. The heavy rain meant that the sky would stay dark until late in the morning; he would stay in the kitchen as the rain pounded onto his roof, and ask himself: What should I do next? Wait through the weekend, telling himself the usual lies about how Sophie would come through with a phone call after all. On Monday, relief at going back to work, surrounded by young people, teaching them how not to be themselves. He would think about her all day and mentally write her a long, candid, passionate letter:

"I thought that insulation matter might become something we could do together. I'm sure we can think of other things to do together. If you're busy, I'll understand, but I would really like to see you again."

He found most of the letter a fake. He did care, and would not understand, about her availability. He mailed her the letter (he could have sent her an email, but that lacked the substance and seriousness of a paper letter with a stamp). She did not reply. He checked his mailbox, knowing she would call or email him, if she did contact him at all. After work, going home and waiting for some sign of her, telling himself it didn't matter. Staying up late, watching insipid TV reruns, not giving up on Sophie because his emotions simply wouldn't let him. After a time, he would decide to take the initiative and contact her. He'd call the local hospitals and ask about her; they would say she hadn't been admitted. He would check the Bayporte online obituaries, to see if she had expired and been written up there. If these measures were futile, he would, with shaking and perspiring hands, call Northup University directly. His secretary, or whoever she was, would say that he was "out of the office," whatever that meant. Had she gone to another city, country, continent? Sophie hadn't been teaching at Northup long enough to make herself so unavailable.

But maybe the young lady would say, "One moment, please," and the next voice he would hear might be Sophie's.

"Hello?"

"Sophie?"

"Yes."

"This is Reg. From the party...?"

"From the party...?"

 Or:

"Reg, with the old house? We need to pick up where we left off. Are you free this weekend?"

That would be far, far worse. At dawn on Monday he put some things into the backseat of his car and drove off into the east.

His intention was just to drive for a couple of days and think things through, then he would go back to his rented house and look at the bedsheets and bottle of wine without wondering about Sophie's doings and whereabouts. He mentally wrote a letter to the community college where he worked, explaining why he needed a leave of absence, and the letter was full of lies, which was why he enjoyed writing it. He had gone without sleep throughout the weekend and had drunk too much wine, and as he loaded his car he thought about how the rest of the world sometimes seemed to gang up on him, especially the women he had loved and believed he could not live without. (He wanted to send Sophie an email saying such a thing, but how would she react? With indifference?) Nobody had a clue about the real Reg: the foolish things he had done, the lies he had told, the money he had squandered. Here was, goofing off again, driving through towns he had never visited, in a hurry to nowhere. By ten in the morning the rain had stopped and Reg started to feel better, in more control of himself, able to push Sophie out of his mind for minutes at a time. There could, and would, be life without her. But the evil, deceitful voices murmured in his head now and again, telling him that Sophie might be on her way to his house, or that his cell phone might buzz with her request that they meet for lunch.

Even if she did call...what then? How long would they last? Eventually he would wake up with her one morning and know *somehow* that things had changed between them, that she lay sprawled on the other side of the bed and her message to him was *Don't touch me*. So much of a man's touching is aggressive; grabbing, not asking. Lying there next to her but unwanted, Reg would want to have some sort of flagrant disfigurement he could blame for her refusal of him. He could blame his whole body, its graying hairs and sagging pouches, worsening each day. He could be

315

dreadful that way, aging, disintegrating. Sophie could never be rejected, her body could never be looked upon with scorn. She would be the one who made allowances, who suggested improvements, who forgave him for being less than she deserved. But for how long?

They might be at a party and Sophie would be surrounded by handsome men, laughing at her jokes and touching her arm, asking for her phone number. Would she give it to them, to these men who maybe could offer her things Reg did not have, and would that be the end of her and him? Of course, it was also possible that none of those things would happen; it was likely, in fact, that their nights together would be full of insulation, fertilizer, wine and giggles. Sophie's absence during that weekend didn't necessarily mean anything except conflicting timetables. Reg kept telling himself this and started believing it, too; every so often he would look for a place to pull a U-turn and head back towards Bayporte. Moments later, bombarded by images of himself, alone and lonely, drunk on wine and feeling sorry for himself as rain beat on his roof, he kept on driving.

When Reg got so sleepy that he feared losing control of the car, he pulled over and nodded off. When it became too cold to sleep in the car, he checked into a motel and slept with the TV on. On the road, he ate at greasy spoons and sat at the counter alongside the truck drivers and prostitutes. Whenever the door swung open, he looked around, half expecting Sophie to enter. His desire to drive, to get away, faded soon. He knew he would go back to Bayporte, and that the farther he went east, the more time he would have to spend going back home. He slept all day and drove all night, and by dawn he was alert and euphoric. He went into a restaurant for ham and scrambled eggs. He stared at the old-fashioned milkshake maker and other items you find only in old places. The slices of pie looked stale. These observations told him that he was returning to his old self, that his love for Sophie was fading. He no longer expected her to walk in on him, and he knew that their plans for his house and backyard would go unfulfilled. He left the restaurant and drove back to Bayporte slowly, for there was no reason to go fast. He checked into a motel and slept with his clothes on and the TV on. He dreamed that the newscaster was speaking to him personally.

He drove and drove. At one point it rained hard and he pulled over to the side of the road, waiting for it to abate. When it did, he continued on his way, feeling more alive, more exhilarated and less crazy than he had in quite some time. Of course, most of the people who knew him would have said otherwise.

Back in Bayporte, he was fortunate. A man called him and said he was casting a project he believed Reg would be perfect for. The project, which was actually a pilot that ideally would become a wildly popular TV series, was about a bunch of American draft dodgers who had holed up in a house on a Canadian island. Reg was to be the star of the show, if in fact the show *had* a star. They would shoot the project on an island near Bayporte; what could be more convenient?

A popular word Reg was hearing then was *ephemeral.* People complained about how ephemeral life was, how ephemeral success could be. Speak for yourself, Reg said. I've lived a hundred years and I'll live a hundred more. He grabbed a hank of his graying hair, as if to emphasize the word hundred. He was already starting to feel like the man he was playing, which he took as a good sign.

...

Months later, maybe longer, Reg was near downtown Bayporte standing on the walkway of the Tyson River Bridge. He wore an overcoat and fedora, and thought he looked like a kind of pimp. He had to look as if he was just minding his own business, while covertly watching the young woman who was contemplating jumping off the bridge. Reg felt glad to be acting again, even though the bitter wind made his eyes water and nose run. The actress playing the would-be jumper tried not to let her teeth chatter. Once they completed this scene, Reg bounded over to the trailer to get some coffee. A woman walked up to him and, smiling, tapped on his shoulder.

"I'm sure you don't remember me. We met at a party," she said. She reminded him of his story about his cat that had jumped off the highrise balcony. Reg laughed and said he recalled her as the person doing a paper or book on mentally ill artists. She no longer looked like the gaunt, doomed aging woman from that evening.

"Shame about Sophie, eh? Tragic."

"What happened to her?" Reg asked, startled.

"She died."

"How?"

"Cancer, they say. But we think it was AIDS."

The woman had to go, and Reg needed to prepare for the next scene. He felt angry and resentful.

Sophie's death somehow failed to register as a tragedy, but he was affronted, his dignity assaulted, by going uninformed of her demise. She had included him in her life for only a short time, and then left him out of her death, denied him the privilege of kissing her goodbye, leaving him to get the dreadful news from an acquaintance on the bridge.

Marge

Back when she ran the store, Marge used to say that she could tell whenever someone was "losing it." Customers would come in and forget why they were there. Or they would come in with their socks on over their shoes. They might come in with tales about being the targets of assassination attempts. Marge said it was genetic, hereditary, as inescapable as cancer. When you got to be too much, they gathered you up and deposited you in the Valley Seniors' Center.

Marge's thing was to do her own cleaning, to save money, and when she got too old and tired to clean, she just didn't do anything. Reg opened her

323

refrigerator door and found inedible items turning different colors. She no longer loaded her dishwasher and her dining table was as sticky as syrup. Reg cleaned it all up for her. Occasionally Marge supervised, leaning from her walker. "What are you mucking around for?"

"Mum, it's me. Reg. I'm cleaning up for you."

"It's plenty clean as it is."

Marge was partly right. Her kitchen had been well organized, at least for her.

"Reg doesn't live here anymore," Marge added, sneering. "He ran off to Bayporte and married some rich hussy."

One morning Reg woke up and went into the kitchen, which looked as if a cyclone had hit it. Marge sat at the table, sipping tea, with pots and pans strewn about. She looked up and said to Reg, "You're the fellow they sent over from Home Care, aren't you?"

"Yes, ma'am."

"Are you from around here?"

"No, I'm from Bayporte."

"Well, I can't afford to pay you."

"Don't worry. Home Care paid me."

Marge poured milk into her tea until the beverage was almost white. Then she sipped at it and made a face.

. . .

Some years earlier, Marge had her house's modest back porch enclosed in glass. That way, despite the weather, she could sit and watch the world go by just as she had sat behind the counter at Marge's Market. The store had long since been boarded over, and the view from the glassed-in porch wasn't much, since it looked out onto a side street. Brandiz, the town across the bridge, continued to be the point of interest for most people, and each year, Marge's house distinguished itself as the disgrace of the neighborhood.

She spent countless hours curled up in a blanket, gazing out at the world she seldom now visited. She covered the wall of the porch with newspaper clippings of infamous crimes by Charles Manson, Clifford Olson and a local pig farmer who had been convicted of luring prostitutes to his farm, then killing them and feeding their remains to his livestock. Reg thought maybe Marge had known the pig farmer, or the prostitutes, or Olson, who had killed eleven children. But Marge, of course, wouldn't say. Back when she needed only a cane instead of a walker, she accepted an invitation from neighbors to drive past the pig farm, which was on the outskirts of Bayporte. They had to ask for directions a few times and when they got there, the two or three cops guarding the entrance shooed them away. No great loss, Marge thought; just an abandoned pig farm with a bunch of cops with latex gloves and Ziploc bags, picking up whatever looked suspicious.

Reg had neglected to visit Marge for a couple of years. He acted when he could, and taught acting when he really needed income. Screen acting, always his top priority, involved many flights to Los Angeles, Toronto and New York. Often, part of his job was doing the talk-show circuit, appearing as a guest on this or that TV show to promote his latest project (as if the project actually were *his,* and not some more famous actor's). During these appearances, he was consistently charming and garrulous, telling anecdotes about the hassles of filming scenes in bad weather, or about the hassles of being a Canadian actor frequently flying to the States (he always called that country by that name, as foreigners usually did). Later, in his hotel room, he wept into his pillow sometimes and kept the TV on because it provided the illusion of having someone there with him, someone with plenty to say (if not always worth hearing).

Marge's home, he knew, was sinking into abject disrepair. Stains from years back wouldn't come out now; smells refused to dissipate and cockroaches corpses lay on the carpet under the beds.

Hate to bother you, know you're busy but this can't wait.

We've been doing our best to look in on Margie as much as we can but she and her house have gotten to the point where they can't be helped by us, good neighbors that we are. Maybe it's time you moved her into the Seniors' Center even if she doesn't want to go. Think about it.

Reg and Paula had both gotten this email. Paula had married a lawyer moved to Calgary. Adept with computers, she worked as a freelance software consultant and traveled nearly as often as Reg did. He rarely saw them but assumed that Paula, no matter where she was, called Marge each night and offered to fly out to Sundown if necessary. Sometimes Paula's husband, Joe, called Marge, wanting to cheer her up with stories about his and Paula's exciting lives. Marge hadn't much use for him and said little on the phone. Yes, she was fine, blah, blah, blah. Yes, Reg calls me, when he gets around to it, but you know how busy he is.

Reg *did* worry about Marge, he went periods of anxiety and obsession over her, but he could go for months without paying much attention to her, too. One period of anxiety had struck him during winter and he drove out to Sundown during a heavy snowfall. Abandoned cars sat at the side of the highway as Reg crept along, his windshield struck by snowflakes as big as quarters. He arrived in the late morning at the house he had grown up in and smiled in spite of himself as he traipsed up the unshoveled walkway and imagined the big welcoming smile on his stepmother's face.

The door swung open and Marge glared at him.

"Move your car!"

"Mum, it's me, Reg."

"I don't care. Move your car. If the cops come by they'll give you a ticket. It's too close to the fire hydrant."

Reg glared back. "If you get an attitude with me, I'll go back to Bayporte right now. Do you understand me?"

"But they'll give you a ticket."

"So what? I'm here, you're here. I've driven a long way just to see you."

"Well, get in here, then. The cold air is blowing into the house."

So he did. Later, he would delight audiences with this story. He could do Marge's glare particular well, and did a nice exaggeration of her bitchy, whiny tirades when she was put in the position of being the object of someone's pity.

...

After reading the Marge-needs-help email, Reg called Paula and Joe, and they urged her to come at once to visit them for a few days. Reg promised himself that he would be on his best behavior. He was convinced that Paula and Joe took a dim view of him and the choices he had made in life. To most people, Reg had succeeded more often than failed, and his failures were memorable and spectacular, which made him that much more ridiculous to Joe and Paula. He thought their concern for Marge would make them less likely to be judgmental towards him on this trip.

He put on a dark jacket, white shirt and dark slacks, then changed into the seersucker suit he'd bought during a trip to Florida. On the taxi ride to Paula's,

Reg again promised himself he would be as crisp and unflappable as any Actors' Studio liar and avoid reviving old disputes with Paula. But his resolve evaporated like a film of sweat once he entered their home and inhaled the unmistakable perfumed scent of his sister. Reg anxiously answered Joe's questions about his work and welfare, and Paula looked at him but not precisely *at* him, as if eyeing something weird and unwanted on her computer screen.

Paula over the years had said, to Reg and others, that she had no use for show business and everyone in it. But she was contemptuous of so many others: painters, musicians, bohemians, political activists, heirs, parasites. She considered Northup's huge, hotly competitive theatre department a colossal waste of money. Reg pleaded guilty to profligacy, decadence, pretentiousness. He did not know if Paula honestly meant what she said, or if she simply felt compelled to attack him. Over the years he had provoked her and she responded; they bickered passionately, red-faced and shaking, and refused to speak to each other for weeks afterwards. Still, Reg knew they loved each other.

But they were powerless to resolve their lifelong rivalry. Which of them was smarter, better-looking, more successful? Each wanted the other's approval, like something promised but not yet given, and Reg and Paula surely took some pride in each other but could not, out of pride or resentment, acknowledge it yet.

"Your mum should have visited us more often," Joe said. A peaceful and tactful man who'd surely wondered at the peculiar family he'd married into, he helped Paula with pouring coffee and clearing the table. "Maybe she should have moved here to Calgary." The few times she visited them, Marge sulked and stayed silent, as if under house arrest. Upon returning home, she boasted of Paula and Joe's big fine home (it was smaller than she remembered and their mortgage was bigger than she knew), their professional success, their great delight in seeing her. Marge thought Reg should envy them.

"I'll bet you wish you had a house like theirs," she said.

"I've had better. Remember Meredith and me in West Shore? I don't miss it a bit." He was telling the truth. He hadn't minded moving out of Meredith's house, although everyone seemed to pity him about it.

After dinner at Paula's, they went into the backyard to enjoy the evening warmth. Reg was proud of his good behavior.

"We should move her into the Seniors' Center. I hear they have better food and lower rates than other places," Paula said.

"I bet she'd be comfortable there," Joe said.

"I could look after her myself." Reg sat back, smiling. Vividly imaginative—his visions were as colorful as a New Mexico sunset—he pictured himself driving to Sundown, installing himself in his old bedroom and assuming total care of his stepmother: cooking special meals for her, taking her for walks, keeping her house clean, mowing her lawn. But he couldn't picture Marge smiling or even nodding thanks.

"Would you like a banana split?" he asked Marge in his fantasy.

"If you have one."

He made the dessert and she gobbled it up, indifferent to the whipped cream and chocolate syrup dribbling from her chin. "Delicious," she said. "Wonderful."

"I'll make you something good next week, too."

"Don't bother."

...

One day, Reg took a tour of the Seniors' Center. He returned with brochures and told Marge about the friendly staff, clean rooms and daily activities.

"I thought you were happy living alone," Marge said.

"It's for *you*, Mum."

"I hate old people. What if you're too sick to go to the dining room? They'd let you starve."

"No, they'd feed you. They'd bring it up to your room."

"What if there's nothing good on TV?" Marge asked.

"You can listen to music."

"What do they have for dessert?"

"Whatever you want."

...

At the Seniors' Center, they had things neatly organized. The spry ones occupied one section, where they played cards, exercised, got haircuts and had day passes. They went to Arts & Crafts and made things; they played to win. They sang songs and took guitar and piano lessons.

In another section, a floor up, more wheelchairs appeared, bad odors lingered longer, more beds were occupied throughout the day and night.

Higher up in the building, some of the residents had given up on life and seemed disappointed when they woke up, or were gently shaken awake, to the news that breakfast was to be served.

I hope she doesn't fight me too much on this, Reg thought.

…

He was sleeping in Marge's glassed-in back porch, which was the only place in the house that didn't reek of its owner. He had been dreaming of her, of chasing her through the Seniors' Center; she could fly, literally, up and down the hallways and elevator shafts. He wanted the staff to help him catch her because the forms hadn't been filled out completely. "We're sorry," they said. "We can't help you until she's been admitted."

He woke up to hear her shuffling about in the kitchen and he felt vaguely disappointed that she hadn't died in her sleep and saved everyone a great deal of trouble. He spent a few minutes staring outside at the gray sky and quiet street, and felt vaguely disappointed that *he* hadn't died during the night.

Reg went into the kitchen and saw Marge sitting at the dinner table, already dressed in a coat, slacks and a baseball cap.

"Are you ready to go?" she asked.

"Where?"

"To that place you've been bugging me about."

"The Seniors' Center. There's no hurry."

"Yes, there is. You came all the way out here to put me in that place. So I'm going to let you have things your way. Let's go."

"We'll go another day, Mum. I'll make you some breakfast. What do you want?"

"I don't want a bloody thing for breakfast. I won't eat it. Let's just go to that place you want to put me in."

Months before the morning Reg took Marge to the Seniors' Center, he had acted in a play videotaped and televised by Canadian public television. His part was minor, but in one scene he had to lay for a few minutes on his stomach, with his buttocks exposed. The scene was supposed to be funny, and the director used a laugh track. Reg didn't mind showing his bare backside to his country, although he didn't think he owned the sexiest butt around. One person who saw the play and was offended by the public display of nudity was Marge, who wrote to the network about the scene, and about how it shamed Marge, her late husband (Reg's father) and all Canadians who had any sense of modesty and decency. Marge's message was an email, and Reg wondered how long it had taken her to write it and how many people had needed to help her. Reg read it to some friends at dinner and got the desired laughs. Reading it to his friends was his way of minimizing its potential to hurt and embarrass him, and at times he did regret all the unresolved disputes and conflicts in his life with Marge. He also realized that those conflicts and disputes were not worth feeling that badly about.

Another time, Reg was to receive an award from a children's charity for his support (he had done little more than pose for publicity pictures). They had invited him to a dinner and ceremony in downtown Bayporte. The charity asked him to provide the name of a relative they could invite as his guest of honor, so he gave them Marge's name and address, believing that she would ignore the invitation but almost hoping the old woman would show up so he could impress her with his circle of admirers.

You see, Mum? You see who I've become? These people all respect me.

Marge ignored the RSVP but arrived at the hotel clutching the invitation. She was stiff and shuffling by then, but still had something left of the straight-backed, dignified carriage Reg remembered. She had always been dressed meticulously and immaculately, if quite simply, but tonight she looked as if she had gone into some cheap ladies' wear store and been dressed by a saleswoman with a cruel sense of humor. As soon as she saw Reg she froze. Marge stared at her stepson as if saying, Well, are you going to come over here, or what?

Marge spoke up.

"Hey, faggot!" she bellowed, as if calling out to some two-legged oddity at the city zoo. Reg, still somewhere in the crowd, forced himself over to greet her. He stood still, a dozen steps away, when he heard her.

She directed her words at Terry, one of the

charity's executives. He looked over his shoulder and, like a B-movie sissy, on the screen to be laughed at, shot her a practiced oh-fuck-off look. Marge, too, looked like an actor in a cult film, wearing a maroon suit with an awkward V-line skirt and paired with a wrinkled, stained cream-colored blouse, an outfit a bag lady might have picked out of a dumpster. On her head sat a thick pink wig pulled over her head like a toque. But Reg, staring at his stepmother as her words echoed in his head like a zealot's blaring voice, saw shock and shame on Marge's face, like a misbehaving child, immediately reprimanded with silence and stony faces, as if the old woman honestly had meant no harm in saying such a thing.

Or had she? You never knew with her, Reg thought. Marge drifted to the back of the room and t communicated only with grunts and nods, refusing refreshments. After watching her sulk for ten or fifteen minutes, Reg asked her if she wanted to go home to Sundown. She said she didn't care, so he asked one of the hotel staff to get Marge a taxi for the TransCanada Railway Station. She would not return to Bayporte.

Reg found Marge's wig during the colossal cleanup of the Sundown house, when Marge was living in the Seniors' Center. He brought it over to her, along with a number of items she had asked for. When Reg was dressed up Marge thought he was one of the doctors, and she said, "You bloody people think you know me better than I know myself." When she saw the wig, she said, "Reg, I don't need a purse, you know. They took all my money."

"Don't you remember this?" he asked. "It's your wig."

"Oh! it's ugly! Did I ever wear it?"

"Once or twice."

"In public?"

"Yes, ma'am."

"I'm surprised nobody laughed at me," Marge said, laughing at herself.

Reg put it on his head and made a cretinous face.

After a time Marge's laughter subsided and she asked, "Are you feeling OK, Reg? Getting on well with Paula and her husband?"

"Yes, fine. Everything is fine."

"And tell your father not to work too hard or he'll end up in a sick bed, just like me."

"I'll tell him, Mum."

"It's good that you're taking care of business."

Then Marge nodded and went into a very, very long

sleep.

What's Your Problem?

As they got older, Reg and Paula, despite their many differences, discovered that they could talk about some things without irritating each other. Their favorite topic was Lincoln Kennedy. They laughed about the time they were both home with chicken pox, and Lincoln walked by and stared at them from the sidewalk for the longest time. Both Reg and Paula sat in the front room and were clearly visible and it was a school day. Lincoln walked right up to the window and looked at the two children, one then the other, then frowned, taking his time in figuring out that these two kids were not at school. He then saw the basketball lying beside the pole holding the backboard and net. Lincoln grabbed the ball and, after a dozen bad free throws, glowered at the ball with the livid frustration of an NBA wannabe.

"Lincoln's playing with our basketball!" Paula screamed.

"I'm sure he won't steal it," said Marge, appearing from another room.

"But Mum, he's *touching* it!"

Reg thought Marge might try to shoo him off. Then he wondered if Marge feared a confrontation. Then he decided that Lincoln Kennedy was every bit as afraid of you as you were of him.

"So what?" Reg said. "He's touched *you* lots of times. He's whispered in your ear. He's kissed your lips."

"He has *not*!" Paula nearly shrieked. "Maybe he held me when I was a baby, but that's all." She turned to Marge and said, "Lincoln never kissed me, did he?"

"No, he did not," Marge replied, although he had held both children.

A custom in Sundown was for Lincoln to visit the Valley Birthing Center and refuse to leave till he whispered a blessing into a newborn's ear. He naturally refused to tell anyone what he said to each child, though it was always the same insipid blessing he'd heard on late-night TV.

Reg held an imaginary infant in his arms and swayed as his lips formed secret words and he blew hot breaths into the child's ear until Paula and Joel, her husband, laughed in spite of themselves. "Reg,"

Paula said. "Come *on*. Don't be so mean." She could tolerate her brother's mockery when he was fairly brief and directed it at easy targets not named Paula.

"Did he *really* do that?" asked Joel, hoping Reg would stop before Paula got mad. You could never tell how far Reg would go once he got started, or how angry Paula might get.

"I don't know." Reg smiled, embarrassed, like a magician forced to pull back his sleeves and open his coat. "I didn't actually see him do it. I saw Gillie Rafelson doing Lincoln doing it."

...

Lincoln Kennedy's main purpose in life, Reg and Paula thought, appeared to be making as ass of himself in public. Sundown loved festivals: Apple Days, the Pine Festival, the Pioneers' Parade and others throughout the year. Sundowners considered it fashionable to complain about feeling an obligation to participate in such affairs, and very unfashionable to admit enjoying the events.

Lincoln Kennedy, present at all of these functions, had an extraordinary gift for physically positioning himself in virtually every picture taken by the Sundowner's photographer, Kenny Johnston. Not that Kenny *wanted* to have Lincoln in the pictures, of course; on the contrary, Kenny, a highly ambitious young photographer who had just graduated from Northup and wanted to get a job at a big American or Canadian newspaper (the Internet hadn't started putting the newspapers out of business). The mayor giving a prize would find that Lincoln's head was between himself and the recipient; Lincoln would make the peace sign in this picture, thumb his nose in that one or even make an obscene finger gesture. Kenny, enraged, could not find one Lincoln-less image. Lincoln, wandering through special events, would stuff his face with free samples, then push children away from the water fountain when he got thirsty. He would hop onto empty stages and speak into microphones; he would whistle with ear-splitting loudness while everyone else applauded a speaker.

Sundown's civic leaders asked each other, What can we do about that little bastard? Why can't we bar him from public events? Why don't we pay someone to chop him up and feed him to the wolves?

They decided no. Lincoln Kennedy resided with his spinster aunts Flo and Sarah, who wouldn't, or couldn't, keep him home while fun things happened outside. If they tried to keep him at home, the authorities feared, Lincoln would fight like a wild animal to get free and join the festivities. Like Odysseus, no amount of bee's wax or rope could restrain him once he'd heard the sirens' song.

"Who's the buffoon?" tourists asked, pointing at Lincoln as he tried to drag people to join audiences he considered too small or hopped onto empty stages to do sound checks.

"His name is Lincoln Kennedy. He lives here. You can't miss him, unfortunately."

"What a simpleton," said Paula's husband Joe.. Reg and Paula weren't sure if the word fit Lincoln. Sundown, a weird place to them, had produced its share of weird people. Lincoln, probably dumber than most people, could read signs and count money; he had yelled at cashiers who tried to shortchange him. Lincoln, Reg decided, lacked emotional maturation.

355

Lincoln's parents had raised him, inadvertently or not, to remain a child until they died, and his two aunts, both hopelessly inexperience in raising children, did little to help him grow up. Perhaps Lincoln had chosen to stay a child, and he fascinates Reg. Lincoln's expressions were not so much those of a moron as of a child going through the terrible twos.

Flo and Sarah were Lincoln's father's sisters. No one found it odd that Lincoln Kennedy would be a name honoring two of America's most famous presidents.Kennedy was a common name throughout Canada, and in their family Lincoln was a fairly common first name, Once he figured out the significance of his name, Lincoln, according to Marge wrote to the Kennedys in Massachusetts, claiming to be one of theirs and asking for an invitation to come out for a visit. He received no reply.

Another story had Lincoln Kennedy masturbating in movie theaters and public urinals. The truth, Reg guessed, might be that he did such a thing once and the stories grew from there. People avoided him on the street and kept their doors locked when they saw him near their homes. If he couldn't get in and nobody inside would speak to him, he would get frustrated quickly and go away.

In his aunts' company, however, he became harmless. He ate bagfuls of chocolate-coated cashews and pecans and happily offered to share his goodies with others, knowing nobody would touch what he had eaten. His aunts took him in for a crewcut every few months and laundered his clothing each week, as if combatting people's stories of what he had done in public.

They must have felt degraded but said nothing.

The sisters were devout Christians whose family had helped build Sundown. Many who knew them, to the extent that one *could* know them, said that they had considered having Lincoln committed somewhere in Bayporte.

"Well, they wouldn't do anything like that. They're good Christian people who wouldn't do that to one of their own."

In other words, they were too stingy. It cost them much less money to keep Lincoln at home with them.

His Aunt Flo taught school in Sundown. She had been there longer than anyone else and everyone respected or feared her. An English teacher, she believed that penmanship was more important than anything else in life. She made her students write down everything. When she told all of her students to copy an entire poem, Reg did not do so, because it was one of his favorite poems and he had already memorized it.

"I didn't ask you if you *knew* it," she said. "I told you to copy it into your notebook. You can't go around considering yourself superior to everyone else just because you know some poetry. What *is* your problem?"

He had been asked that question throughout his life and considered it rhetorical. What was his problem? He supposed he had many problems, but so did everyone else.

. . .

Reg and some other brand-new Sundown High School graduates were invited to the Kennedys' home for a slideshow of the sisters' missionary work in

Calcutta. Their slides, decades old, had deteriorated; still, Reg assumed that India hadn't changed much from those grainy images flashing on the wall: decrepit buildings, dirt roads, brown-skinned, emaciated natives who all looked alike. Reg thought the Indians' poverty happened due to cultural historical forces he probably would never understand.

But Ms. Flo did not see things that way.

"The Indians are terribly misguided people," she explained. Ms. Sarah, shy and docile, operated the projector. "They have a hundred religions, yet they lack the only one that matters: Christianity." Ms. Flo meant, of course, that Christianity alone could eliminate the Indians' poverty.

Afterwards, the ladies served delicious, homemade cookies, cakes, sandwiches, punch. In a dark corner, Lincoln huddled in a blue serge suit, white shirt and red tie. Much of his clothing was already dotted with crumbs. Maybe that was why people arrived each year, not to see the slides of India, but to eat the wonderful food and behold crazy Lincoln in his own habitat, stuffing brownies, pecan bars and salmon sandwiches into his mouth. The sight of his bald head, jiggling jowls and protruding stomach must have disturbed and fascinated those people, as if they were allowed to sit by and stroke a tranquilized bear or wolf.

...

In Sundown, Christians gradually lost their power, but that erosion happened so slowly that the Kennedy sisters didn't know or pretended it wasn't so. Church attendance declined, but the two old sisters' big house still had a portrait of Jesus staring you down in the main entryway. Their house, overfurnished, overheated, overblessed, sent a message that Reg interpreted as, *Look after Him and He'll look after you.*

Some bad things, though, happened to the Kennedys. The sisters' big mistake came in drafting a petition compelling the Canadian Radio and Telecommunications Commission to immediately terminate programming "that promoted the decline of Canadian civilization." They left it up to the authorities to decide what programming they meant. The Valley Church of God, not the sisters' church, had the most bodies on Sunday, so the Kennedys set up a table with the goal of asking parishioners to sign their petition.

Marge said that the sisters had installed Lincoln Kennedy at the petition table with the simple but crucial job of handing the gold-filled Parker ballpoint pens to signers and collecting the pens once the signature was completed.

The problem was in leaving Lincoln sitting there with two expensive pens. He amused himself by sticking the pens up his nose and making walrus noises. Passersby guffawed at him and shook their heads. Flo and Sarah hurried over, gathered him up, pulled the pens out of his nose and stuffed their petition into their shopping bag.

"The Kennedy sisters never got over that," said Marge. "No one ever took them seriously anymore." Marge smiled, and it was hard for Reg to tell exactly what about the Kennedys' disgrace pleased her. Probably all of it.

Gillie Rafelson, Reg's first love, a smart-alecky girl, did the imitation of Lincoln Kennedy. Like Reg,

Gillie went to school because she had to, and she wanted nothing more from public education than to have some fun and get through it all quickly. Gillie, for most of the time Reg knew her, had clowned it up. Neither of them had come to school well organized or conscientious; they came missing supplies or with homework undone; each day presented an emergency along such lines. Their crises brought them together.

They sat side by side, giggling and kidding around. Reg came in late to find Gillie entertaining a group of classmates with her Lincoln Kennedy imitation. He frowned, unable to remember that bit of her *schtick* and rather hurt that she had decided to do Lincoln for these others publicly rather than do it for him privately.

Gillie, a natural comedienne, made these kids

double up in red-faced hilarity as she found Lincoln's awful face, his uncoordinated movements, his furious, hushed words. Years later, while watching Joan Rivers, Ellen Degeneres and other women, Reg would think, *You missed your calling, Gillie. You were funnier than those women on TV. You could have made millions.*

After a time Reg didn't see her at all, even passing on the street. He learned that she had joined the Canadian Army and been shipped off to Afghanistan. He tried to picture Gillie in a green uniform, carrying a machine gun, guarding poppy fields, keeping the peace. He sometimes had trouble accepting the fact that he, she and the other Sundown kids had grown up and become men and women, people who did things like get married, have children and fight in Afghanistan. Things that freaked him out.

...

Marge's Market closed because of its owner's arthritis. Marge, for a while, still felt well enough to attend casino nights and Bingo games. Reg went to Sundown sometimes and asked her about her evenings out. Did she ever see the people he knew, his classmates, the local folks…?

"Oh, there's just that smart-alecky girl you were so fond of. Gillie Rafelson. She's around."

Reg's heart skipped a beat. "Gillie? She went into the military. Peacekeeping in Afghanistan, right?"

"Yes, well, she got pretty banged up over there, so they sent her back home. Her rehab went on and on. She had to learn to walk all over again."

"Jeez…"

"Don't be so sorry for her. I understand they gave

her quite a pension. *Quite* a pension." Then, "Yes, she's still around. She finds ways to fill up her days, like the rest of us. She used to have the devil in her, could make fun of people just to make you laugh."

"She used to make fun of Lincoln Kennedy."

Marge slapped her thigh. "Oh! There's a name I haven't heard in a while! Lincoln Kennedy! He's still alive. They finally got him into a home or something in Bayporte."

"I guess he doesn't make the rounds anymore with the festivals and things," Reg said.

"You *have* been away," Marge said. "They quit doing those festivals and special events. Too much money to put them on. People change, towns change. People stay in now. They watch TV and fiddle with their computers."

"Where does Gillie live?"

"Don't know, but you'll not have much trouble finding her if you look around a bit in the local hangouts. Gillie was looking around for some part-time work. Not volunteer, you understand. *She* would have to get a paycheck for her trouble. She figures she gave so much of herself to the military overseas, from now on she expects that she's gonna get paid to pee. Gillie's nice, I always liked her, but she was too bloody cheeky. Everything was a joke to her. Always smirking. People think she was smirking at them."

...

Reg thought for a minute about Lincoln Kennedy, whom he pictured as a silent old man wanting nothing but junk food and a TV set to stare at. Reg guessed that old folks' homes were full of people from your past if you looked hard enough, not that he wanted to do any such thing.

He was in a hurry to return to Bayporte, but would stay in Sundown until he could get Marge's house cleaned up and listed with a realtor. But her neighbors from down the block came by, insisting that he join them at the Legion Hall downtown, so he with them to Sundown's most popular place for people who wanted to forget their troubles.

Men sat at card tables, playing poker. Reg walked around and looked at the framed photographs covering the wall. Pictures of guns and airplanes, the men who used them. A very male thing, to fight the wars and hang the framed memories on the walls. WOMEN MAKE LOVE, MEN MAKE WAR. Bumper sticker wisdom. Reg again felt grateful for being in a country without conscription.

He had hardly felt a moment's desire to serve in the Canadian Army and could scarcely place Afghanistan on a map. Let some other poor bastard die on the battlefield.

"I've seen you on TV," said a woman whose husband sat at one of the card tables.

"That so?" I'm so famous now, he thought, that they recognize me even in Sundown.

"You look more human in person than on TV," she said.

"It's not cheap, making me look so fake." He told her about studio makeup, lighting and the dozens of takes the director wanted.

"Here's Gillie," the woman said, smiling and making way for the frail, graying woman who held a pint of beer as if it were a golden elixir. Reg felt badly at first because of her physical deterioration, then instantly felt better because he'd wanted her so badly for so long, and now saw that what he'd wanted in her had disappeared. Gillie seemed, literally, "not all there." He could tell that she had lost her irresistible sassiness and playfulness, as if they were tangible items that had tumbled out of her Army backpack. Her dirty blonde hair that used to fall into her face had turned to silver wire, and she pulled it back with some effort. Reg observed her anxious, restless movements. Her blue crewneck sweatshirt struck him as too austere for the younger Gillie.

But of course the younger Gillie had gone, left somewhere in Afghanistan or elsewhere.

In the Legion Hall they were talking about who had died, was dying, or who had been put into a financial predicament by a family member's recent death.

"They want you to probate wills now. Everyone's got to do it, and even the lawyers goof it up sometimes. Even when you're dead they're still shaking out your pockets and your body's not even cold yet."

The man who said that was playing cards with other men at a table. Everyone nodded.

"You don't actually *live* here, do you?" asked the woman who had made room for Gillie.

Reg said he lived in Bayporte but seemed to spend half his life elsewhere, making personal appearances and taking acting roles in California and Toronto.

"I envy you," said the woman.

He reminded himself that once he got back home, he needed to make an appointment for lunch and sex. That was how he saw it: Appointment. Lunch. Sex. He was having an affair with Tammy Norgaard, another man's wife. They had known each other for years, had fallen in and out of love but remained friends. After their romp, they would sit up in bed, eating Chinese takeout food from the carton. They did much eating and drinking after sex. Reg knew, somehow, that he was sharing Tammy with someone else in addition to her husband, but in their world it was impolite to ask about those matters. Tammy's husband had a girlfriend. Reg and Tammy had met through Meredith, and Tammy's interest in the Dunsmuir heiress was so keen that Reg felt Tammy would rather have become Meredith's lover. But

Meredith and Reg seldom saw each other. They had a daughter in common, but little else, and he believed their girl was losing interest in him. Meredith's girl, not his.

Reg and Gillie stared at each other for the longest time. They both knew why they had become friends and why they still felt a strong bond to each other. They wondered why they had let a little thing like war interfere so much with their marvelous friendship.

"Have you done Lincoln lately?" Reg asked.

"What?"

"Lincoln Kennedy. You used to imitate him for me."

Gillie smiled. "No, that was just for you."

"Is the old bugger still alive?"

"If he is, they've locked him up somewhere."

"Remember how he lived with his aunties, and they had those parties, and served us those goodies?"

She nodded. "Lincoln wore his refreshments well. I wonder what those old biddies would think now of India and China. They're taking over the world."

Reg meant to regard her as his long-lost sister, separated by years, geography and war, but still his sibling. He wanted to remind her of Johnnyboy and Dee Dee Rae but Gillie probably didn't want to hear about them. Reg knew Gillie wanted him to say something to her but she would give him no clues about what to say. *He* wished he could restore her good health and girlish exuberance. That was what friends were for, he decided. Friends or siblings, or whatever they wanted to be to each other.

Much later on, Reg remembered how frustrated he felt by seeing Gillie again. He was overcome with empathy and compassion for her, although he had done no hand-holding with Gillie; she would have resented him for being condescending. He had walked away from that visit with her feeling that he had somehow failed her in an elusive but significant way. He had often felt that way about his years as an actor, unsure if the "zero" he had gone to was the right one, or if he had emphasized the most meaningful words, made the most powerful gestures, kissed his female opposite with sufficient passion. He viewed many areas of his life this way: flawed moments, unsaid words, awkward exits. His visit with Gillie? He could have done better.

Reg did not tell Paula or her husband any of these

things when recalling Lincoln Kennedy's antics or Gillie's exploits. He also deliberately neglected to tell them that Gillie had died, which he learned from the *Sundowner* online. He read it every day, and suspected he was about the only person who did so. He had bought Marge a laptop computer after she complained that everyone else in Sundown had one, and when he got her one she managed to surf the Internet and found the *Sundowner*. She said that reading words on a glowing screen gave her a headache, and she never touched the computer again. But that was where he found out about Gillie Rafelson.

Ms. Gillie Rafelson, Lieutenant, of Sundown suffered a fatal stroke while attending an event at the Canadian Legion Hall. An accomplished and dedicated career officer, Lt. Rafelson served with distinction in Afghanistan and other locations.

He did a Google search but could find nothing more about her. Just the usual blah-blah the military said about one of its own, especially a good-looking woman with a dazzling smile. Gillie looked like a movie star in the image next to her notice. The Canadian military would make sure to bury her with full honors.

Reg decided not to tell anyone about her, mostly because the item said very little and he had nobody left in his life to tell. and his listener probably would fail to appreciate her anyway. All he could say about Gillie Rafelson was that he had loved her like a brother while wanting to love her like a lover.

ABOUT THE AUTHOR

George Onstot was born in San Francisco but has lived in Vancouver for a number of years. Currently he is at work on his next novel.